THE SPECTRE BRIDEGROOM AND OTHER HORRORS

MORE WILDSIDE CLASSICS

Dacobra, or The White Priests of Ahriman, by Harris Burland
The Nabob, by Alphonse Daudet
Out of the Wreck, by Captain A. E. Dingle
The Elm-Tree on the Mall, by Anatole France
The Lance of Kanana, by Harry W. French
Amazon Nights, by Arthur O. Friel
Caught in the Net, by Emile Gaboriau
The Gentle Grafter, by O. Henry
Raffles, by E. W. Hornung
Gates of Empire, by Robert E. Howard
Tom Brown's School Days, by Thomas Hughes
The Opium Ship, by H. Bedford Jones
The Miracles of Antichrist, by Selma Lagerlof
Arsène Lupin, by Maurice LeBlanc
A Phantom Lover, by Vernon Lee
The Iron Heel, by Jack London
The Witness for the Defence, by A.E.W. Mason
The Spider Strain and Other Tales, by Johnston McCulley
Tales of Thubway Tham, by Johnston McCulley
The Prince of Graustark, by George McCutcheon
Bull-Dog Drummond, by Cyril McNeile
The Moon Pool, by A. Merritt
The Red House Mystery, by A. A. Milne
Blix, by Frank Norris
Wings over Tomorrow, by Philip Francis Nowlan
The Devil's Paw, by E. Phillips Oppenheim
Satan's Daughter and Other Tales, by E. Hoffmann Price
The Insidious Dr. Fu Manchu, by Sax Rohmer
Mauprat, by George Sand
The Slayer and Other Tales, by H. de Vere Stacpoole
Penrod (Gordon Grant Illustrated Edition), by Booth Tarkington
The Gilded Age, by Mark Twain
The Blockade Runners, by Jules Verne
The Gadfly, by E.L. Voynich

Please see www.wildsidepress.com for a complete list!

THE SPECTRE BRIDEGROOM AND OTHER HORRORS

Edited by

R. Reginald
and
Douglas Menville

WILDSIDE PRESS

To Barry Levin, Fellow Collector and Good Friend.

THE SPECTRE BRIDEGROOM
AND OTHER HORRORS

This edition published in 2006 by Wildside Press, LLC.
www.wildsidepress.com

THE SPECTRE BRIDEGROOM.

In one of those beautifully romantic spots, so often met with in the Hartz Mountains, at the sight of which, the ancient days of chivalry and romance, with all their dark terrors and knightly achievements, rush so powerfully on the mind, stood the lordly castle of Count Rudolph von Swartzburg. It hung frowning over the brink of an inaccessible precipice, surrounded by misshapen piles of dark granite, which seemed to rear their craggy heads, tufted with matted clusters of gloomy pine, beech, and oak, as if in defiance of the huge mass of towers which weak man had dared to raise as rivals in their own awful solitudes.

The count had for some time entertained, with all that generosity and hospitality so well according with the chivalric notions of those days, a cousin of his, the Count Albert von Sinnern. This gay and high-minded youth was passionately fond of the chase, and scarcely a day elapsed, without himself and his cousin passing the greater portion of it in hawking in the vicinity of the castle; the country, by its deep, woody recesses and hilly situation, being particularly adapted for this noble pastime.

Albert had a favourite falcon, which engrossed so great a part of his affection that he seldom or ever lost sight of it, and after a day's sport, with many endearments, he reluctantly resigned it to the care of the falconer. It actually appeared as if the little creature understood the gestures of its fond master, and endeavoured to repay, as well as to deserve, his kindness, by its superior dexterity in pursuit of game.

Unfortunately, this bird, through the carelessness of the falconer, disappeared one morning. Distracted by the loss, Albert searched, though ineffectually, every spot in the neighbourhood, and would gladly have sacrificed all his remaining hawks and hounds to have once more obtained possession of his lost favourite.

One day, after having spent many hours in fruitless search of this remarkably beautiful creature, Rudolph and himself, enticed by the fallacious hope of succeeding in their pursuit, became more and more entangled in the lone haunts of the mountains. Rudolph reminded him how very unsafe it was to await the approach of night in so wild and dangerous a spot; but so intent was he on the subject of his wanderings, that he entreated Rudolph to return to a hut hard by, and there await his arrival, promising that no great time should elapse ere he returned.

At such a time, and situated as they then were, it would have been little short of madness to have left his friend alone, so they continued to proceed together. "Do you not hear," joyfully exclaimed Albert, as the sun's last rays were fading slowly from the summits of the distant hills, "there he is! there he is!"

The sound really appeared to proceed from the bells of a falcon; and Albert thinking himself already in possession of his favourite, began to entice him by the kindest expressions: but in vain; the sound seemed to recede as they approached, and to mock all their endeavours to reach the spot from whence it arose.

Like a chamois, Albert climbed the most pathless tracts, and it was with great difficulty that Rudolph could follow him. They soon attained the summit of such a hill, that it was found utterly impossible to advance, and, unfortunately, equally so to recede. "Good God!" exclaimed Albert, looking over the sides of a steep and perpendicular cliff, "is it possible that this can be the way we ascended?"

Rudolph was amazed; but it could not have been otherwise, as not the least vestige of any other path was visible. To return was out of their power, as the first step towards a retreat, would certainly have been the last on this side of the grave.

Mute with astonishment, and confounded at the terrific situation in which they had placed themselves, they wildly gazed around. And as evening began to spread her shadowy veil over the surrounding scenery, their situation became more and more alarming, and to add to the horror of the scene, they distinctly heard the wolves prowling in the vicinity for their prey.

It may easily be imagined, that they lost no time in searching for an outlet; but this proved ineffectual. The broad cliff on which they stood, appeared to them totally separated from all the neighbouring hills; and they began to suspect, that they had arrived there through the agency of some mischievous demon, the peasantry in the environs strongly affirming the reality of such supernatural occurrences.

It must be owned, that the thoughts of remaining the whole night in such a dangerous spot, and seeing no hope of the morning being any alleviation to their sufferings, was not very consoling. Strange as it was, even in this terrible situation, Albert did not forget his falcon; but often expressed his ardent desire of having him once more in his power.

The night grew darker and darker, when suddenly they thought they perceived a light at a short distance; they were not mistaken in their conjectures, and their astonishment passed all bounds on its approaching still nearer, as if by a regular pathway; at last they heard footsteps close at hand.

The most beautiful figure had perhaps never afforded more real pleasure to the two young friends than the hideous features of the deformed lantern-carrier did at the present moment, while she, on her part, appeared much surprised to find them there. "Well, my good old dame," exclaimed they, "how did you manage to ascend this rugged rock?"

"I might with more propriety ask you that question," replied she; "I am at home in these wilds, but you do not seem much accustomed to such rough lodgings."

"And where live you?" they further enquired.

"In a hut not far from hence."

"In a hut, and to whence a path from this leads?"

"Certainly," answered the old woman; "so if you fear to pass the night here, follow me." Such an offer, and at such a time, could not be refused. "I will light on before," said she; "now turn neither to the right nor left, but tread in my footsteps."

They followed the lantern according to her directions. Though not quite even, the way was tolerably passable, and they were rather surprised that they had not before discovered it. It was true, the branches of the trees tended much to conceal it from casual observance, and they often found some inconvenience in wading through the wide-spreading boughs that crossed their path. All this could not efface the thoughts of his main object from Albert's mind. "Have you perchance seen a stray falcon hereabouts, my good dame?" said he.

"Yes," replied the conductress, "I have; was he not very large, with ash-grey wings and dark spots?"

"You are right!" exclaimed Albert, scarcely knowing how to express his delight; "that must be my dear falcon; oh! what would I not give if it were mine again!"

"Who knows what may happen?" said the old lantern-bearer; "the whole of yesterday we heard the sound of his bells in our neighbourhood; once or twice he flew close by the hut; my daughter, who was struck with his beauty, attempted to lure him in, but he refused the proferred bait, and soaring majestically aloft, was soon lost to our feeble sight; but, perhaps, she may have been more lucky to-day."

"Woman!" cried Albert, "you might ask much for that bird."

"My wishes," she replied, attempting a smile, "know no very great extent; you must make your terms with my daughter."

The party now proceeded onwards without any

material change, over craggy steeps, into the most precipitate dells, and again up the sides of the most stupendous heights. At length, overcome with fatigue, they stopped awhile to gather a little breath. " Stay, old woman," cried Rudolph; "you told us your dwelling was not far; pray, what do you call far, if this is not so?"

" What! tired already, good gentlemen?—well, only a few steps further, and you may rest yourselves; close under that hill lies my cottage."

" The hill exhausted their remaining strength; but upon seeing a flame ascend from a grotto by the side of the hut, they renewed their efforts, and arrived at last, ready to sink from excessive exertion.

"That is my daughter," said their conductress, pointing to a young female who proceeded from the mouth of the grotto.

" How very long you have staid this time!" exclaimed the girl; " I have expected you this hour."

" As an excuse for my absence, I have brought two guests, who were too unaccustomed with the path to follow me at my ordinary pace."

Albert and Rudolph were struck with astonishment at the brilliant beauty of the daughter; they had thought such serenity of countenance, regularity of features, and symmetry of figure, could alone have proceeded from the chissel of the Grecian sculptor, and could scarcely believe their own eyes when they beheld a human being, arrayed in dazzling white, standing before them, in the midst of such a wild solitude, in all the beauty of a goddess. She appeared to them as if adorned for the altar, and only awaiting the arrival of her bridegroom to lead her thither. The fashion of her dress also differed widely from the neighbouring costumes.

While Rudolph was trying in vain to find a single point or feature about this wonderful being, that could at all authorise the idea of so close a relationship as existed between her heavenly figure and the deformed, dirty, old hag that gave herself out as her mother, Albert stood transfixed before her; and for the first time since he had quitted the castle, he seemed to have quite forgotten the falcon.

The blissful beam of her dark eye had totally bewildered his senses; unwittingly he spread his open arms towards her; she advanced a step, and her bashful downcast eye soon completed what its tender glance had begun.

"Christallina," said the old woman, who had observed all that had just passed with seeming pleasure, "the falcon we saw yesterday, belongs to this gentleman; perhaps you have succeeded in making him a prisoner to-day."

"Yes," returned she, "but not to give him up so soon again. You would not," addressing Albert, "give me all I require for it."

"All," exclaimed Albert, "but most willingly myself, and all I possess."

"Your riches, sweet stranger, have no charms for me; it is yourself I ask, yourself alone, and for ever!"

Rudolph felt terrified by the earnestness of her words, particularly when he saw the deep impression they made upon Albert. "Thine I will be, and for ever!" exclaimed he, as he exultingly clasped Christallina in his arms, and held her to his bosom, as if willing she should remain there to eternity.

His friend was much struck by the singularity of the whole proceeding; to give himself up to an unknown and highly mysterious being, was a madness that only those who were present and beheld her superhuman beauty, could at all excuse; and nothing, indeed, but that beauty could have justified in the least the precipitate step he had taken. It would have been useless to remonstrate at such a moment, and his friend hoped to be better able to enforce his advice in the morning, when the first wild burst of passion should have subsided. For this reason he hid not touch on the subject when they retired to the room which had been allotted to them for their night's repose.

Rudolph was too fatigued to remain long awake; but the rising sun found Albert still pacing the chamber with agitated step and disordered air;

he confessed that he had been wandering about the house during the whole night, and that only the earnest entreaties of Christallina, and her repeated threats of never seeing him again, prevented his approaching her chamber.

"God be praised!" cried Rudolph; and after a friendly expostulation, he succeeded in showing him the folly of his yesterday's mad conduct, in a proper light, and after some time was delighted to see his remonstrances take a salutary effect on the disturded mind of Albert. He threw himself on Rudolph's bosom, and so far perceived and repented his thoughtless levity, that he was even willing to give up his dear falcon, rather than fulfil the engagement he so thoughtlessly made the preceding evening.

These resolutions appeared to be firmly made, and were much strengthened on the appearance of the loathsome old woman, who now brought in their breakfast. "Good God!" exclaimed Albert, after she had retired, "that such a wretch was within an ace of becoming my mother-in-law, and by my own consent."

They could not, however, help feeling disquieted by the thought that Christallina might keep him to his promise; and were considering the best method of evading it: but their fears on that head were misplaced; for the old woman soon re-appeared, to their surprise, arrayed after her fashion, in sumptuous apparel.

She told them she came from her daughter, who awaited them, either to fulfil her engagement with Albert, or to give him back his promise; for she thought it would be wise to avoid every appearance of precipitancy in such a weighty affair. Overjoyed at these assurances, and from such a quarter, they followed her to the grotto, from whence her daughter came forth to meet them.

Her appearance the evening before was but a faint reflection of the lustre her beauty and celestial figure shed around at present. And as her ruby lips opened, and her dark swimming eye, the true pledge of love and ardent passion, flashed on Albert, his cousin, with intense sorrow, saw at once all his new-formed resolves consumed in that glance.

"Handsome stranger!" said Christallina, whilst a smile of ineffable brightness, that lit up the whole of her lovely countenance, played on her lips, "I owe, perhaps, your promise of yesterday to the earnest desire you expressed of obtaining your favourite. My love for you knows no bounds, and it therefore requires a love as ardent and sincere in return. I require all, or nothing! Go, sweet stranger, leave me, and never let me see you more, or consent to become wholly mine for ever!"

"Your's in life, your's until death!" cried Albert, prostrating himself before the beauteous girl. She raised and pressed him passionately in her arms; then slowly lifting her lovely eyes, depressed from a sense of her open confession, they suffused a beam of joy and happiness over Albert's manly countenance, that seemed almost divine.

The old woman then said to Rudolph, in a tone that bore a strong resemblance to Christallina's, "Man, be thou witness of the blessing I deal to this pair;" so saying, she placed her hands upon both their heads, exclaiming, "Woe be to them and their's, that turn my blessing to a curse!"

Rudolph stood petrified, for she spoke the last words in so dreadful a tone, that even Albert started from Christallina's arms to gaze upon her, and the glance that met his, gave rise to such an inward sensation of horror, that his trembling frame could scarcely support him. But the soft and enchanting sound of Christallina's voice soon re-assured him. "Now," said she, "youth of my soul! you shall have your redeemed falcon,—go and bring him, mother." She went, and very quickly returned with the bird on her hand.

Albert burst forth into an extravagant cry of joy at the sight of his long-lost darling; and when he had secured him on his wrist, fondled him with expressions that proved how delighted he was at having at last attained the object of his tedious search.

It now became every moment a matter of much greater wonder how these two beings, in this uninhabited wild, should possess all the articles of comfort to be met with in civilized society. "Who are you?" asked Albert, "and how do you live in this lone place?"

"Those, my love," replied Christallina, "are short questions that require long answers. My birth-place is now no more of this world: the waves of the northern ocean, on which it was for some time borne, have received it in its depths again. As to any further intelligence, you must have patience until a fitter opportunity."

Albert then began to think of returning to the castle; and upon offering to take Christallina with him, "No," said she, "go to your home, and think of me. Come as often as you please to visit me; but I cannot consent to live with you in your habitations; it would only serve to remind me of a still greater splendour I am doomed to miss." A look from Albert seemed to ask an explanation; but she shook her lovely head and left them.

As soon as Albert had recovered from the surprise which the mysterious behaviour of Christallina had thrown him into, he begged to know the best way out of the forest. The old woman now volunteered her services, which were gladly accepted; and when they were ready to depart, she led the way; at times winding through thick underwoods, at others cut through by mountain torrents that came tumbling down from their sources, dashing their foam from rock to rock, at once impeding their progress, and not unfrequently rendering it unsafe.

Albert, quite out of patience, asked their conductress, if she knew no better road. " Not by day," said she; " but I will be at the castle-gate with my lantern, every night at nine o'clock, at your service."

" At the castle?" cried Albert, in the greatest astonishment; " why, woman, you know not its distance from hence."

" Fear not," replied she, a ghastly smile overspreading her haggard features, " those who are well acquainted with the path as I am, will easily find the way." So saying, she left them to pursue their route alone.

They gazed long in wonder after the mysterious hag, and neither seemed willing to interrupt the silence that reigned around.

When they arrived at the hut where they had intended to sleep, all its inhabitants participated in their joy at the recovery of the beloved falcon, although much astonished at their nightly ramble in those unfrequented parts. " You ought to bless your stars," observed an old peasant, " that you have escaped without danger; with many it is otherwise: and those who are lucky there may easily lose their road to salvation."

" Do you know with any certainty what is likely to befal one there?" enquired Albert, while a deadly paleness overshadowed his fine countenance.

"I know nothing, nor do I wish to know any thing," replied the peasant. They now took up their guns, and left the cottage.

The conversation that had passed there, did not seem at all calculated to restore the young men's gaiety; and Albert had at most but a few words for his falcon. At length, seizing Rudolph by the arm, he exclaimed, deeply agitated, "Friend of my soul! could it have happened otherwise?"

What could Rudolph answer, when he remembered well his own feelings at the time Albert's resolution vanished before Christallina's superhuman beauty.

After some time they arrived at the castle, to the great joy of their friends, who began to entertain some fears as to their safety. Indeed, a party of domestics had been formed for the purpose of searching through the forest, and only awaited further orders, for setting out.

From this time Albert became quite a different man: and it required an explanation, such as Rudolph alone could give, to acconut for the sudden change in his behaviour, and to comprehend how his former youthful gaiety could, in the eyes of his friends and the world, be superseded by that gloominess of spirit which now sat so heavily upon him.

He soon began to suspect that the falcon from

the hills was not his own, although the falconer, glad to escape the well-merited blame for its loss, persisted in its identity. Albert was himself at first of the same opinion; but he became every day more doubtful. He now felt satisfied, from repeated observations, that this falcon had oftentimes, something so terrific about him, that he was obliged to turn from him and his maddening gaze to escape contagion.

He was now nearly always absent from the castle alone. Those who had formerly enjoyed his society and shared the pleasures of the chase with him, could not satisfactorily account for the change they perceived, but contented themselves with reflecting that time would unravel the mystery. The neighbours, also, had of late remarked the nightly watchings of the old lantern-carrier, and being all more or less given to superstition, they at once decided that something alarming would happen to the inmates of the castle; for they firmly believed that some forest-fiend had began his evil work.

After some time had elapsed, Albert seemed partly to have regained his wonted cheerfulness, although his time was still divided between his hawks and hounds; but still his present joy had a something about it that nearly bordered on madness, while his usual confidence was entirely withdrawn from Rudolph.

One day, on his return from the chase, he

threw his arms around his cousin's neck, crying, "Friend, and more than brother, I have proved myself unworthy of your friendship by the most abominable connections; but my unhappy lot still entitles me to count upon the pity of a relation. I have now for some time past paid nightly visits to Christallina, and the lantern-bearer is still my guide; our route differs each time, which prevents the possibility of my ascertaining the proper road. All is mystery, and I fear dark, unhallowed mystery; but I am resolved to break this dreadful spell."

Albert now seemed overcome by the intensity of his feelings; and it was some time before he sufficiently recovered to proceed. But his cousin kindly soothed his troubled mind, and he thus continued: "Christallina still persists in concealing her birth and parentage from me, and remains quite firm to the first account of the sunken island, telling me, her father was a prince who sought refuge there from misfortunes. Whether this be true or not, I cannot take upon myself to determine; but I must ever look upon her and the old hag who stands in her service, as two awfully mysterious beings."

Again Albert paused; but soon after resuming the conversation, he said, "It is utterly impossible that this old woman can be the mother of Christallina; her beauty is every day new, and that it is which serves to distract me; for although her features visibly change, they still retain that fascination, which first allured me from my duty: but since yesterday, I hold her in such utter abhorrence, that I am quite resolved never to see her again."

"Then," said Rudolph, "I fear you must discovered something that gives you reason to hold the peasants' tales concerning her not altogether unfounded?"

"It is but too true," replied Albert; "but there is a dark and fearful veil drawn over all that relates to her; and, woe to me! I am but too deeply entangled in the mazes of her hellish mysteries; but," added he, suddenly springing up, "I dare not repeat them."

After these words, Albert went to the falconry. In a short time, Rudolph's attention was attracted by a loud triumphant langh. He went to the window, and found it proceeded from Albert. He was staring at the falcon he held in his hand with an infuriated eye, while the animal at his last gasp, and bleeding from a wound he had inflicted, appeared to return his gaze with equal fierceness; he dashed his murdered favourite to the ground, and rushing into the room, exultingly exclaimed, "Thank God, I have now one demon less to deal with!"

To such a burst of seeming frenzy, Rudolph had nothing to reply. As they stood together by the window, the falcon still stirred beneath the grass, when Albert put an end to his sufferings, by ordering him to be covered with a large stone. What occasioned the greatest astonishment, was, that the old lantern-carrier did not appear that night at the castle; they began to suspect she must be acquainted with the death of the falcon, and on that account remained absent.

Evening succeeded evening, and the old hag came not. The violence exercised upon the bird, seemed to have broken all the former ties that existed between Albert and the inhabitants of the lonely hut, He considered himself now entirely free from their power, and that his present abode might not awaken any unpleasant sensations with respect to his former unhappy connexion, as also with the hope, that change of scene might tend to obliterate those recent circumstances from his mind, he determined upon leaving Rudolph's castle for his own domains immediately.

His castle, in point of situation, could not be surpassed; and the surrounding scenery was sufficiently diversified to delight every one whom business or pleasure brought thither. Within bow-shot, on the one side, the blue ocean expanded itself, at times reflecting the countless luminaries which studded the vaulted arch of heaven: and at times rearing its billowy head, far above the mountain-tops which, on some parts of the shore, formed an impassable barrier.

At times like these Albert would walk on the

castle terrace, and watch the elementary war. To him there was music in the awfully-rolling thunder,—and the lightning darted and flashed without exciting even a sensation of terror in him. He seemed most happy when thus engaged, for he could not, in the moments of quietude, erase from his mind the recollection of the old lantern-bearer and her mysterious daughter.

Time, which effaces all things, at length restored something like serenity to Albert's mind, and he occasionally accepted the invitations of his friends, who felt happy to discover that the social feelings he once possessed had not quite forsaken him. On other occasions he would join in the pleasures of the chase, and return home, apparently happy.

From the castle he often corresponded with the Count Rudolph; and in one of his letters, acquainted him with his intention of espousing a cousin of his, for whom he had long cherished an affection.

One evening when Count Rudolph was present at an entertainment given by a neighbouring nobleman, he was struck by the appearance of a beautiful woman, in splendid attire; he was surprised at the striking resemblance she bore to Christallina in all respects. Her extreme beauty attracted universal notice; and upon making enquiries relative to the mysterious stranger, he was told, she went by the name of Marchesa di Terrenci.

The entertainment drew towards a close, and the company began to disperse. After the crowd was in some measure diminished, she approached him, addressing him as follows—" You, Count Rudolph, have not, I presume, lately heard from your friend, Count Albert?"

" No," answered he, " I have not, for some time past."

" Then," said she, " I can tell you, that he has returned to his castle, and as far as appearance goes, he seems happy; but they who think so, know not his heart. He is about to enter into a matrimonial engagement with a relation of his; but woe be to him and his intended bride! If he dare to accept her hand, be assured, my vengeance, which those who once feel forget not easily, shall sooner or later overtake him. The cruel death of the falcon," added she, " although it tore him from my heart, could not protect him from my revenge." So saying, she disappeared among the crowd, and was seen no more that evening.

Upon further enquiry, the Count found that nobody was acquainted with her, neither knew they from whence she came, or whither she went, after her sudden departure from the entertainment. Rudolph, awed by the solemn manner in which she addressed him, and fearful lest disastrous consequences should follow such a warning, lost no time in communicating what had happened to Albert, entreating him as he valued his own safety and the happiness of his intended bride, to delay the solemnization of the nuptials for a short period.

Unhappily the letter came too late for Albert to benefit by its contents. He had already led his lovely cousin Clara, in all the bloom and beauty of youth, to the altar. She had been brought up at a neighbouring convent, and since her mother's death, had been received into her aunt's family, where she was looked upon in the light of a daughter.

Albert had seen her frequently there, when he visited the family, and a mutual affection having sprung up between them, they were united by the consent of her guardians, who gave a sumptuous entertainment on the occasion. After spending a short time at his uncle's house, and receiving the congratulations of his friends and acquaintances, he took his leave, and conducted his lovely bride to his castle.

Count Albert, young and handsome, possessed something so noble and commanding in his countenance, so affable and fascinating in his address, that it was not to be wondered that Clara became deeply enamoured of him; and she hoped in his love and protection to ground all her future prospects of happiness. Alas! poor girl, how much was she deceived!

Though possessed of many noble qualities, Albert had imbibed a wildness and ferocity from his occupations and former roaming life, that ill accorded with the mild disposition of his gentle mate. These circumstances, therefore, naturally embittered her anticipated dream of bliss. Count Rudolph's ill timed communication, visibly affected his conduct towards her.

He now more than ever wandered about in the hidden recesses of the forests with his hawks, seeking in vain to dissipate the fearful forebodings that pressed heavily on his mind. On his return late in the evenings, his cold and repulsive manner, added to the dark terror of his contracted brow, caused his wife to shuddder at his presence, and in some measure to fear him.

One evening, the waves of the ocean were moaning along the shore, and the land-birds were screaming with unusual melancholy; a storm seemed to be gathering fast, and Clara's gentle bosom heaved high, for she well knew her husband was from home, ând with a wife's timidity feared the worst. She could not imagine what induced him to frequent the gloomy recesses of the forest; for he did not seem to sport there.

At length the storm burst upon the castle; the thunder, peal after peal, shook the building to the foundation, and as the lightning darted among the trees, it appeared to set the forest in a blaze. Clara's heart sickened; she knew not how to compose herself; she wandered from one apartment to another, and after a little time repaired to the castle chapel; reverentially she kneeled before the altar, and fervently invoked the author of all good to protect her husband, and guide him safely to her longing arms. She arose and left the holy place with a calmer mind, and retraced her steps to the drawing-room, anxiously awaiting the arrival of her beloved lord.

A loud knocking at the gate announced Albert's arrival, and the domestics hastened to testify their joy at his safe return, but he heeded them not. After changing his apparel, which was drenched by the storm, he entered the apartment where Clara awaited him. Overjoyed at beholding him, she exclaimed, "Thanks, gracious heaven! he is safe." Albert started, and withdrawing himself from her embrace, paced the room with agitated step.

Clara tried her utmost skill in endeavouring to soothe his troubled spirit, but in vain; and in reply to her remonstraces, as to his not frequenting the chapel at the usual times of service, he answered roughly, "What should I do there?"

This circumstance sank deeply on the mind of Clara, and gave rise to sad forebodings; Albert continued his visits to the forest, and spent but little time at home. One evening, her apprehensions were renewed, as her husband generally returned at that time, and she was used to see his tall shadow glide along the wall of the summer-house in which she retired to read, expanded to a giant shape, as reflected by the rays of the setting sun. His return in itself always conveyed an indescribable feeling, but the dreadful shadow had now something so terrible in it, that she would run to the window to convince herself that her husband had not in reality assumed so hideous a form as the shadow represented.

One evening in particular, she was more than usually appalled by the reflected appearance. It came not as it was wont to do with slow and pensive step, but glided across the wall with a quickness she had never before witnessed. Upon rising to ascertain the cause of this extraordinary occurrence, she saw her husband turn the corner; contrary to custom, he did not proceed to the falconry, but came with a quick and agitated step, the bird still on his wrist, directly towards the spot she had retired to.

"Clara, my dear wife," cried he, an ashy paleness overspreading his convulsed features, "prepare, prepare yourself for the worst!" He had scarcely uttered these terrible words, when a woman, wrapped in a black veil, entered the apartment, and, going up to Clara, quickly unveiled herself.

"Your husband," so began the unknown, reddening, "your husband has been guilty of a crime against me, as well as yourself; I am, and still continue to be, his first and lawful wife. Consider then," added she, with a sarcastic sneer, "in what light I must look upon you!"

"Count Albert," said the justly-irritated Clara, "it is for you, not me, to answer this woman, to tell her who we are, and how we stand connected."

"Spare your pride until a fitter opportunity," retorted Christallina, "you see by his trembling how little he is in his proper place."

"Vile woman!" exclaimed Albert, "do you accuse me of want of courage, you, who by hellish arts have ensnared my soul. Avaunt! malicious demon! I defy your machinations. This woman is mine by the approbation of the holy Church, and mine she shall ever remain."

"Clara," vociferated the enraged Christallina, "beware, and dread my vengeance; for both your sakes, break off all further connection with him."

"Never!" replied she, "that I will not, dare not do. It belongs rather to you to relinquish that which never has been, and never can be yours."

"You have pronounced your own sentence," cried the infuriated Christallina, her eyes beaming with such an unnatural fire, that Clara shuddered to meet their gaze: "mine he shall remain, even in death, whilst you must content yourself with his shadow." With a bitter smile, she seized the Count and dragged him from the room.

Clara vainly attempted to cling to him, her strength failed her, and she sank senseless to the ground. Her aunt was much shocked to discover her in this situation, and it was some time before Clara could communicate to her the dreadful scene that had just taken place. Poor Clara was totally insensible to any consolation her aunt attempted to afford her, who after remaining with her for some time accompanied her to her chamber. There she fell into a deep reverie, which, from her excessive agitation, soon gave way to a quiet slumber.

In a short time, she was suddenly awakened by a rustling noise against the wall, she thought she heard her husband, according to custom, hanging his night watch up there. "God be praised!" she exclaimed, "you are safe returned at last, dear Albert." She received no answer. Again she distinctly heard the clothes of his bed lifted up, and some person lay down in it. Trembling with affright, she called on him again; but still no answer. She then sprang up, took the shade from the night-lamp, and with a wild and terrified glance, searched the chamber throughout; but still she saw nothing. She now took up the lamp, and tottered to Albert's bed. Oh! what words can describe the icy chill of horror that crept over her agitated frame, when she discovered the bed empty and untouched, and the watch she had so lately heard against the wall not in its place!

The cold dews of fear sat on her pallid brow, and pervaded her trembling limbs, as she stared wildly on the lonely bed, and the dreadful presentiment of evil darted across her mind. She had scarcely extinguished the lamp, and returned to her bed, when she again heard a noise in that of her husband's; she listened attentively, and distinguished the loud breathing of a person sleeping; it became every moment stronger. She sprang to Albert's bed with the full conviction of finding him there, when, to her inexpressible terror, all was lone and still as before.

Although nobody appeared to be in the bed, she lifted up the clothes with a palpitating heart; it was empty, and in complete order; and it was this dreadful order, combined with the foregoing mysterious circumstances, that almost occasioned the loss of her senses. The horrid thought now occurred, that her husband must be dead, and that this was the shadow with which Christallina had threatened her, come to deceive her with the fond hope that it was Albert himself.

To her bed she dared not return, and shuddering even at the thought of remaining alone in the fearful chamber, she left it; but although she closed the door after her, the loud noise of a sleeper still rang in her ears, and followed her as far as the three rooms through which she passed. At length, in an agony of superstitious horror, she threw herself at the foot of a crucifix, erected in a small recess, in a distant apartment, and there poured forth her soul in fervent prayer until the morning light burst through the windows of the room.

He aunt, terrified at not finding her in her chamber, had followed her thither, and not knowing the cause of Clara's dismay, was shocked at the deadly paleness of her face, and the hollow wildness of her eyes. She descended with her, and tried to soothe her by every consolation and kindness in her power. But Clara soon found, that even the day was to have its peculiar horrors.

After breakfast, of which she partook to avoid the appearance of singularity, she sprang up suddenly, exclaiming, "Ah! there he is at last."

"Who?" demanded her aunt.

"My dear, lost husband," frantically replied she; "do you not hear him?" Upon this she rushed into the garden, calling upon her dear Albert, and searching for him in every recess of its winding alleys; but receiving no answer, she returned wringing her hands, and sank into her chair in a perfect state of insensibility.

She had experienced the same deceit as on the night before, and heard Albert's voice, busied in the falconry, only she thought the cries of the animals were more piercing than usual. Her friends, persuaded as to the madness of her assertions, vainly attempted to overcome her fears by every argument in their power. She was too certain of the terrible reality, to be convinced she was in error; and taking a book, was left once more alone to meditate on the late extraordinary occurrences.

The cries of the falcons and hounds, with the occasional chiding voice of her husband, continued distinctly throughout the day; but as often as she hastened down in the fond expectation of meeting him, so often was she cruelly deceived, for not even a trace of what she heard was to be found.

Until this time she had avoided the summer-house, from the scene that had taken place there, with all its direful consequences, being still fresh in her memory; but as it could not be more terrible to her than her own chamber, she retired thither towards the evening. The shadow, that she had before so much dreaded, she now prayed for as a blessing, as she knew it must be the forerunner of Albert's happy return. "Alas!" said she, sighing, when the sun had just reached the point at which it usually appeared, "alas! to-day I fear the dark resemblance will not come to warn me of his much-wished approach."

The words had scarce died on her lips, when the gigantic shadow stalked in a bent, and melancholy attitude across the accustomed wall. She then with heartfelt joy sprang to the window, stretching out her arms more to welcome the sight than to protect her from its approach. She hastened to the wall, that she might not be again deceived; the shadow had not yet passed, and with her hands before her eyes, dreading to search for that she most wished to find, she precipitately left the room.

In an agony of suspense, Clara now sought relief by walking on the castle-terrace; she knew her husband had often delighted to walk here, and she fondly hoped to meet him. Alas! her hopes were vain, nought but the shadow could she see. Overcome by her feelings, she was about to quit the spot, when she met Count Rudolph, to all appearance just arrived from a long journey.

"O Rudolph!" exclaimed the agitated Clara, "have you seen my husband?"

Rudolph took her hand, and gazing on her mournfully, broke by degrees the dreadful news that Albert had expired in his arms at eleven the night before, at a strange inn, where he had by chance found him; and that he just came in time to soothe the last moments of his dying friend.

A dreadful shudder thrilled through Clara's veins, as she called to mind that eleven was the hour when she first heard the rustling noise in her chamber. With a faltering voice, she asked, how Albert had spent the last minutes of his life.

"At his earnest request," replied Rudolph, "a priest attended him, at the sight of whom, the mysterious stranger, who tore him from your arms, departed enraged, showering imprecations on the head of her repentant victim. Through me, he entreats your forgiveness for the past, in the hopes of which he departed in peace."

"Forgive him," cried Clara, bursting into an agony of grief, "yes, that I do, from my heart; it would ill befit a sinner like me to withhold forgiveness from one, who after a life of misery and woe has been mercifully received into the bosom of his Creator, through a timely repentance, and reconciliation with the holy church. You, my dear friend, have, and ever must, retain my warmest thanks for your kindness."

"And now," said Rudolph, "let me give you some few last lines from him you hold so dear. I should not have interrupted your unfeigned sorrow, by presenting them now, had it not been the dying request of poor Albert."

"Why not!" replied Clara, stifling her grief, "all that comes from him must be dear to me: give me the letter." She opened it with a trembling hand, and having bedewed it with a stream of tears, read as follows:—

"Dear Clara,

"I die in hopes of your forgiveness, and therefore die happy. How well could the bearer repay you for all the pain and anxiety I have caused; believe me, my love, I should leave this world with less regret did I know you safe in the love and protection of my friend. Farewell, my beloved wife, I trust we shall meet hereafter.

"ALBERT.

"Count Rudolph," said the weeping Clara, "although my husband's wishes must ever be dear to me, I have still more sacred duties to perform. At present, I can give no decisive answer. My heart, torn by such a succession of fearful incidents, knows not at present how to decide; but you shall hear from me soon."

The effects of the exasperated Christallina's threat did not, however, cease to pursue their intended victim, and worn down by terror and grief, she at length sought refuge in the convent at which she had been brought up; and after a time, recovered a portion of that serenity of mind and calmness of spirit, which a pious observance of holy exercises never fails to pour as a balm on the wounded soul; but she never was wholly herself again.

Of course, Clara refused the offer of Count Rudolph's hand, although she held him in the highest esteem. She felt convinced that her heart had been too much wrung, ever to love him as a husband should be loved. Rudolph remained a short time at the castle, aud then returned to his own residence.

Poor Clara lived many years at the convent in peace, beloved by the Abbess, who having been a particular friend of her deceased mother, cherished her as a daughter, and admired by all those who knew her, as well for her kind and benevolent conduct, as for her mild and unassuming manners.

FINIS.

DEAN AND MUNDAY, PRINTERS,
THREADNEEDLE-STREET.

THE DEMON HUNTER
OR,
THE WHITE WOLF OF
THE HARTZ MOUNTAINS

Anonymous

OR,

THE WHITE WOLF OF THE HARTZ MOUNTAINS.

In the early part of the seventeenth century, there lived, on the borders of Transylvania, an Hungarian nobleman of high rank and extensive possessions, but whose moral character did not accord with his elevated position in society. The steward of his estates was one Hugo Krantz, and although a serf, was by no means either illiterate or poor. In fact, he possessed considerable property, and it was his intelligence and respectability of character which led to his elevation to the stewardship; but under the feudal system, which then prevailed

No. 42.

in the Austrian dominions, whoever was born a serf remained so for ever, even though he became a wealthy man.

Hugo Krantz had been married five years when our tale commences, and had three children, two boys and a girl. His wife was a very beautiful woman, but unfortunately more beautiful than virtuous; she was seen and admired by the lord of the soil, who immediately resolved that she should become his mistress. The steward was sent upon a journey to a distant farm, and during his absence, his wife, flattered by the attentions and won by the assiduities of the count, yielded to his wishes. The intrigue could not be long concealed from Krantz after his return, and in a short time he suspected it. He watched his wife, and soon had incontrovertible evidence of his dishonour, for he surprised her in the arms of her seducer. Exasperated to the highest pitch of resentment, and quite losing the mastery of his passions, he snatched a gun from the wall, shot his wife dead, and dashed out the brains of the count! Aware that as a serf, not even the provocation he had received would be allowed as a justification of his conduct, he hastily collected what money he could lay his hands upon, and fled from the scene of his double crime, taking his three children with him. As it was in the middle of a winters night when the murders were committed, he was far away before they were discovered; but knowing that he would be pursued, and that he had no chance of escape of he remained in any part of his native country, he continued his flight through Germany until he found himself in the wild solitudes of the Hartz mountains.

There he fixed his abode, with his three children, in a rude, yet comfortable cottage, on the borders of one of those vast forests which then covered the northern parts of Germany; around it were a few acres of ground which Krant cultivated, and which, though they yielded but a scanty harvest were sufficient for their support. The woods were infested with bears, wolves, and wild boars, in the pursuit of which he passed much of his time in the winter, when the children were obliged to remain within doors for safety. He had purchased the cottage and the land about it of one of the rude foresters, who gain their livelihood partly by hunting and partly by burning charcoal, for the purpose of smelting the ore from the neighbouring mines. It was distant about two miles from any other habitation; the bleak mountain side above was studded with dark pines, and below was a wide expanse of forest, on the topmost boughs of whose trees they looked down from the cottage, as the mountain below rapidly descended into the distant valley. In the summer, the prospect was beautiful; but during the severe and dreary winter, a more desolate scene could not well be imagined.

Every morning, during winter, Krantz shouldered his gun, and left his cottage, locking the door, in order to prevent the children from straying into the forest. He had no one to assist him, or to take charge of the children—indeed, it would not have been easy to find a female servant who would have lived in such a wild solitude. The poor children were sadly neglected, and suffered much in the winter, when, owing to his fears of an accident, he left them without fire, and they were obliged to crawl under the bearskins to keep themselves warm.

The adventurous, and often hazardous, existence of the hunter was in keeping with his restless mood; either from remorse for having committed murder, or from the misery consequent on his charge of situation, or both combined, he was never happy but in activity. Children, when left much to themselves acquire a thoughtfulness not common to their age. So it was with the children of Hugo Krantz, who, during the short cold days of winter, would sit silent for hours, longing for the happy days when the snow would melt, and the green leaves burst out, and the birds begin to sing, and when they would again enjoy their liberty.

One evening, when little Marcella was five years of age, and her brothers seven and nine respectively, Krantz returned home rather later than usual; he had been unsuccessful in the chase, and the weather was very severe, and many feet of snow were on the ground, he was not only very cold but in a very bad humour. He had brought in wood, and the children were blowing the ignited sticks into a blaze, when he pushed the little girl aside roughly, and she fell against a stool, and cut her mouth. Hugo, the eldest boy, raised her up, and the three children withdrew into a corner, afraid to venture near their morose and unkind parent. Krantz drew his stool nearer, muttered some expressions of ill-humour and discontent, and heaped on more wood. A cheerful fire was soon blazing on the hearth, but the children did not, as usual crowd round it. They continued to crouch in the corner to which they had retired, and Krantz hung over the fire gloomily and alone.

Thus they sat for about half-an-hour, when the howl of a wolf, close under the window of the cottage, fell on their startled ears. Krantz sprang from his seat, and seized his rifle; the howl was repeated—he examined the priming, and then hastily left the cottage, shutting the door after him. The children listened anxiously, for they thought that if he succeeded in shooting the wolf, he would return in better humour; and although he was harsh to all of them, and particularly so to little Marcella, still they loved their father, and liked to see him cheerful and happy, for who else had the poor things to look up to? And here we may observe, that no children could be fonder of each other than were those of the hunter Krantz; they never quarrelled, and if, by chance, any disagreement ever arose between Hugo and Herman, their sister, a lovely and amiable child, would kiss them both, and by her intreaties and winning manners restore peace between them.

"Our father has followed the wolf, and will not be back for some time," said Hugo, when they had listened for some time, without hearing the report of their father's gun. "Let us wash the blood from your mouth, Marcella, and then we will leave this corner, and go to the fire and warm ourselves."

They did so, and sat by the fire until near midnight, every minute wondering, as it grew later, why their father did not return. They had no idea that he was in any danger, but they thought that he must have chased the wolf for a very long time.

"I will look out and see if father is coming," said Hugo, going to the door.

"Take care," said Marcella, timidly. "The wolves are about now, and we cannot kill them, brother Hugo."

Hugo opened the door very cautiously, and but a few inches, and peeped out; but he could see nothing but the dazzling snow and the tall pine-trees. So he closed the door, and rejoined Herman and his sister at the fire.

"We have had no supper," observed Herman. in a tone which implied that he thought it would be very acceptable; for Krantz usually cooked the meat as soon as he got home, and during his absense the childrens had only what remained from the previous night's repast.

"And when our father comes home after his hunt, brother Hugo," said

Marcella, "he will be glad to have some supper; let us cook it for him and ourselves, and keep it hot till he returns."

Hugo climbed upon a stool, and reached down some venison, from which he cut some slices, and proceeded to cook them as he had seen his father do. The venison was dressed and he was putting it upon platters before the fire, to keep hot until their father returned, when they heard the sound of a horn. The children looked at each other, and listened; they heard footsteps on the crispy snow, and a rustling among the brown leaves of the forest, and in a few minutes the door of the cottage was opened, and Krantz entered, ushering in a young female and a tall dark man of middle age.

Before describing his guests more particularly, we will relate the circumstances under which he had met with them. When he left the cottage perceived a large white wolf about thirty yards from him; but as soon as the animal saw him, it retreated slowly, growling and snarling. The hunter followed; the wolf did not run, but always kept some distance in advance of him, now stopping to growl defiance at him, and then trotting off again. Thus the chase went on for some time, Krantz not choosing to fire until he could take a sure aim; and being anxious to shoot the animal, (for the white wolf is very rare,) he continued the pursuit for several hours, during which the wolf led him higher and higher up the mountain.

There are certain spots in the Hartz mountains which are believed by the hunters and miners of the district to be the haunts of evil spirits; and one of these spots, an open space in the pine forest above his cottage, had been pointed out to Krantz as dangerous on that account. These spots are well-known to the hunters, who invariably avoid them; but, owing either to his not being a native of the district, and therefore less liable to be influenced by its legends, or to his superior education, Krantz disbelieved the stories he had been told, and followed the white wolf to the place of evil repute without hesitation. On reaching it, the animal slackened her speed, and turned round; Krantz approached, raised his gun to his shoulders took deliberate aim, and was about to pull the trigger, when the wolf suddenly disappeared.

He thought at the moment that the snow on the ground must have dazzled his sight, and he lowered his gun from his shoulder to look for the animal; but it was gone—how it could have escaped, where the ground was clear of trees and bushes for some distance, without his seeing which way it had gone, was beyond his comprehension. Vexed at the ill success of his chase, he was about to retrace his steps, when he heard the distant sound of a horn. Astonishment at such a sound, at such an hour and in such a wild solitude, made him forget his vexation and disappointment for a moment, rivetted him to spot. In about a minute the horn was blown a second time, and sounded much nearer; Krantz stood still, and listened, and after another interval of about a minute, it was blown the third time.

Krantz knew that the note which had been blown was a signal that the party was lost in the forest; and just as he was about to shout, in order to guide them to him, he beheld a man on horseback, with a young female seated behind him, enter the cleared space, and ride up to him. For a moment he called to mind the strange stories he had heard of the supernatural beings who were said to haunt certain spots in the Hartz mountains, but on the nearer approach of the parties, a glance satisfied him that they were mortals like himself.

They were well apparelled, and the coal-black steed which the man bestrode was of matchless symmetry. The man was tall, robust in form, and apparently about fifty years of age. His long black hair, however, was not at all grizzled by age; though there were some deep lines in his swarthy countenance. The expression of his countenance was stern, but his dark eyes were as bright as any fair lady could desire to behold, and his teeth were white and even. His attire was that of a hunter, but of good materials, and silver gleamed upon his horn and on the hilt and sheath of his hunting knife.

His female companion, who seemed about twenty years of age, wore a travelling dress of dark cloth, deeply bordered with white fur; the body was tight, and set off to advantage a form of surpassing symmetry and peerless grace. A profusion of flaxen ringlets, as glossy and soft as the finest silk, fell from under a cap of ermine, and flowed over her sloping shoulders and superbly developed bosom. Her complexion was exquisitely fair, her teeth faultlessly white and even, and the general effect of her features pleasing and fascinating. Her eyes were blue and very bright, but there was a restlessness in their expression, and sometimes a furtiveness in their glance, which was apt to produce an unfavourable impression.

"Well met, friend hunter," said the stranger, addressing Krantz, as he reined his steed close to him. "You are out late, the better fortune for us. We have ridden far, and are in fear for our lives, which are eagerly sought after. These mountains have enabled us to elude our pursuers; but if we find not shelter and refreshments that will avail us little, as we must perish from hunger and the inclemency of the weather. My daughter, who rides behind me, is more dead than alive even now."

"My cottage is only a few miles distant," returned Krantz, "but I have little to offer you beyond shelter from the weather and the comfort of a fire; to the little I have you are welcome. May I ask whence you come?"

"Yes, friend," replied the stranger. "It is no secret now; we come from Transylvania, where my daughter's honour and my own life were in equal jeopardy."

This information was quite enough to create an interest in favour of the strangers in the breast of Hugo Krantz. He thought of his wife's seduction, of the tragedy that followed, and of his own flight from his native land. He immediately and warmly repeated his hospitable offer, and added to it a promise of all the assistance and protection in his power.

"There is no time to be lost, then, good sir," said the stranger. "My daughter is chilled with the frost, and cannot hold out much longer against the severity of the weather."

"Follow me, then," said Krantz, leading the way towards his home. "I was lured away in pursuit of a large white wolf, which came to the very window of my cottage, or I should not have been out at this time of the night."

"The creature rushed by us just as we came out of the forest," observed the female, in a soft and silvery voice.

"I was nearly discharging my piece at it," said Krantz; "but since it has been the means of enabling me to do you a service, I am glad that it has escaped."

In about an hour and a half, during which Krantz led the way at a rapid pace, the cottage was reached, and the stranger dismounted, assisted the female to alight, and followed their conductor in.

"We are in good time, it seems," observed the stranger, catching the odour of the broiled venison, and walking up to the fire, and surveying the children, he added, "you have young cooks here, friend."

"I am glad that we shall not have to wait," rejoined Krantz. "Come, mistress, set yourself down by the fire; for you need warmth after your cold ride."

"Have you any place where I can put my horse?" enquired the stranger of Krantz.

"I will take care of him," replied Krantz, and leaving the cottage, he led the animal into a shed, in which he was accustomed to keep fuel.

The young female had now seated herself near the fire, and beckoning the children to her, spoke kindly to them, and caressed them; that is, Hugo and Herman, for Marcella would not go near her, but slunk away, and hid herself in the bed, without waiting for the supper, which, half an hour before, she had been so anxious for.

Krantz soon came in, and placed the supper on the table, of which the strangers partook heartily. When the meal was over, he requested that the young lady would take possession of his bed, and he would remain at the fire, and sit up with her father. After some hesitation on her part, this arrangement was agreed to, and the children crept into the other bed, which was in the room where their father and his guest were sitting. But the poor children could not sleep; there was something so unusual, not only in seeing strange people, but in those people sleeping at the cottage, that they were bewildered. Poor little Marcella, who seemed afraid of them, was quiet, but she trembled during the whole night, and seemed at times to repress a rising sob. Their father had brought out some brandy, which he rarely drank, and he and the strange hunter remained drinking and talking before the fire.

"So you come from Transylvania?" observed Krantz.

"Yes," replied the hunter. "I was a serf to the noble house of Ottoschatz my master would have had me surrender my fair girl to his wishes—so I gave him a few inches of my hunting-knife, and fled for it."

"We are countrymen, and brothers in misfortune, then," observed Krantz, taking the hunter's hand, and pressing it warmly.

"Indeed!" exclaimed the stranger. "Are you then, from that country?"

"Yes; and I, too, have fled for my life," replied Krantz. "But mine is a tale too melancholy to tell."

"What is your name?" enquired the hunter.

"Hugo Krantz."

"Hugo Krantz!" repeated his guests. "I have heard your story; you need not renew your grief by repeating it now. We are kinsmen, then; though we have never met before. I am William Barnsdorf, your second cousin; how strange that we should meet in a hut on the Hartz mountains!"

They filled their horn-mugs to the brim, and drank to each other, after the German fashion. The conversation was then carried on in a low voice; the children were awake, eager to catch the slightest whisper so much was their curiosity excited, but all they could collect from it was their new found relative and his daughter were to take up their abode in the cottage, at least for the present. In about an hour, they both fell back in their chairs, and appeared to sleep.

"Marcella, dear, did you hear?" said Hugo, in a low and sad tone.

"Yes," replied Marcella in a whisper. "I heard all. Oh, brother Hugo! I cannot bear to look at that woman—I feel so frightened."

Hugo said no more, and in a few minutes the three children were fast asleep. When they awoke the next morning, they found that the hunter's daughter had risen before them. The night's rest had refreshed her, and she looked more beautiful than ever; but the children regarded her with sidelong glances of suspicion and aversion, and evidently considered her an intruder. She spoke kindly to them, and patted Marcella on the head, and would have kissed her; but the child slipped away from, and slunk into a corner, trembling all over.

We need not linger upon this portion of our narrative. Wilfred Barnsdorf remained three weeks at the cottage, during which he and Krantz went out hunting daily, leaving Christine, the Transylvanian's blue-eyed daughter, with the children. She performed all the household duties, so that the cottage soon presented a much greater degree of comfort than it had ever worn before; and she behaved so kindly to the children, that the dislike they had conceived towards her was overcome, and even the aversion of little Marcella by degrees wore away. But upon Krantz the effect of her fascinations was still greater; for he had conceived a violent, and apparently insurmountable aversion to Women, after the terrible tragedy which had compelled him to fly from his native land; and even this had dissolved before the radiant charms of Christine Barnsdorf. The hunter and himself slept in the room which Christine had occupied on the night of her arrival, and another bed had been prepared for the Transylvanian in the outer apartment, in which the children slept. Wilfred usually retired as soon as he had dispatched his supper, and Krantz and Christine remained by the fire, conversing in low tones for hours afterwards. Their glances revealed the secret of their hearts, and sometimes Krantz would look towards the children's bed, to see if they were asleep, and then imprint a kiss upon Christine's glowing cheek or moist red lips.

"Cousin Wilfred," said he, one day, when his guests had been three weeks under his roof, "I love your daughter, and would wed her; she reciprocates my affection, and all that is required is your consent."

"You may take her, Krantz, and my blessing with her," returned Wilfred. "I shall then leave you, and seek some other habitation; it matters little where."

"Why not remain here?" said Krantz.

"Go, no, I am called elsewhere," replied Wilfred. "Let that suffice, and ask no questions; you shall have Christine."

"I thank you for her, and will duly value her," returned Krantz; "but there is one difficulty."

"I know what you would say," said Wilfred, after a moment's pause, during which Krantz looked upon the ground. "There is no priest in this wild country; true—neither are the laws much observed. But there must be some ceremony, or I shall not feel easy. Will you consent to be married after the formula that I will prescribe?—if so, I will marry you directly."

"I will," replied Krantz.

The hunter then called Christine into the room, and after acquainting her with what had passed between them, desired Krantz to take her by the hand.

"You must take a solemn oath," said he, as they joined hands. "Say then, after me—I swear, by all the spirits of the Hartz mountain—"

"Nay, why not by the blessed saints, or the Trinity?" said Krantz, interrupting him.

"Because it is not my humour," replied Wilfred. "If I prefer that oath, less binding, perhaps, than another, surely you will not thwart me?"

"Well, be it so, then," returned Krantz. "Have your humour; but I cannot see why you prefer that I should swear by that in which I do not believe."

"Yet many do so, who profess to be devout Christians," rejoined Wilfred. "Please yourself; will you be married, or shall I take my daughter away with me?"

"Proceed," said Krantz; and he repeated after the hunter the following oath:—

"I swear by all the spirits of the Hartz mountains, by all their power for good or for evil, that I take Christine Baansdorf for my wedded wife; that I will ever protect her, cherish her, and love her; and that my hand shall never be raised against her to do her harm. And if I fail in this my vow, may all the vengeance of the spirits fall upon me and upon my children; may they perish by the vulture, the wolf, or other animals of prey; may their flesh be torn from their limbs, and their bones blanch in the wilderness; all this I swear."

Krantz hesitated as he repeated the last words; little Marcella could not restrain her feelings, and as her father repeated the last sentence, she burst into tears. This interruption discomposed the party, particularly Krantz; he spoke harshly to the child, who stifled her sobs, though the tears continued to course each other down her fair cheeks.

Such was the second marriage of Hugo Krantz. The next morning the hunter mounted his coal-black steed, and rode away through the glades of the now leafless forest. There was an almost immediate change in the behaviour of Christine towards the children; she no longer spoke kindly towards them, and in the absence of their father, she often beat them, particularly little Marcella, whom she would often gaze upon with an expression in her eyes that made the child shudder.

One night, Hugo and Herman were awakened by their sister, for they all slept in one bed. Marcella was trembling very much, and they saw by the moonlight that penetrated the boughs of trees without, and shone in at the window of the cottage, that she was very pale.

"What is the matter?" said Hugo.

"She has gone out," whispered his sister.

"Gone out!' repeated Hugo and Herman together.

"Yes, gone out at the door, in her night clothes," replied Marcella. "I heard the inner door opened gently, and looking up, I saw her glide across the room lift up the latch quietly, and go out."

What could induce their step-mother to leave her bed, and go out in her night-clothes, in the middle of winter, when the snow was lying deep upon the ground? The children asked themselves and each other this question, but were unable to answer it. They remained awake, and in about an hour they heard the growl of a wolf, close under the window.

"There is a wolf," observed Hugo. "She will be torn to pieces!'

In a few minutes, however, the door was opened with noiseless caution, and their step mother appeared, clad only in her night-dress, as Marcella had stated. She closed the door very quietly, washed her face and hands, and then entered the inner chamber. The children trembled and wondered, but soon fell asleep; and were afraid to mention, on the following morning, what they had seen.

"What has made this water bloody?" inquired Krantz, when he went to wash himself.

"It is what I washed the deer's head in last night," replied Christine.

Now, it happened that the children had seen her throw away the water in which she had washed the deer's head, and this falsehood to which she had given utterance so increased their suspicions, vague and undefined as they were, that they resolved to watch her. The result was that on several nights, and always at about the same hour, they observed her quit the cottage in her night-dress; after she was gone, they invariably heard the growl of a wolf under the window, and they observed that she always washed her hands and face, on her return, before rejoining their father. They observed, also, that, though she ate little at meals, and sometimes with apparent repugnance, when she was preparing the meat for dinner, she would often furtively put a raw piece into her mouth, and eat it with evident relish.

The fears and suspicions of the children increased, and Hugo, who was a bold spirited boy resolved to follow their step-mother out, and endeavour to solve the mystery of her nocturnal wanderings. Herman and Marcella endeavoured to dissuade him from this project which appeared to them full of danger; but he would not be controlled, and one night laid down in his clothes, to be prepared to follow her as soon as she went out. About midnight, the door of the inner room was cautiously opened, and Christine glided in, clad only in her white night-dress, which gave her something of a ghost like appearance, notwithstandiug the unnatural brilliance of her eyes and the feverish flush upon her cheek. She glanced towards the children, who appeared to sleep, and then she gently opened the outer door of the cottage, and went out.

Hugo immediately jumped up, got upon a stool to reach his father's gun, which was loaded with ball, and opening the door as quietly as Christine had done, slipped out after her. Marcella trembled for her brother's safety, and Herman was anxious and uneasy. After the lapse of a few minutes, they heard the report of a gun, which caused Marcella to utter a cry of terrot, but did not awaken Krantz. The children trembled and looked at each other without speaking. In about another minute Christine re-entered the cottage; her countenance evinced anxiety and terror, and there were stains of blood upon the lower part of the skirt of her night-dress.

Marcella would have uttered a cry of terror, had not Herman had the presence of mind to put his hand over her mouth, though he was greatly alarmed himself. Christine opened the inner door gently, and looked in; and seeing that her husband was still asleep, she glided across to the hearth, and stooping down, blew the embers of the wood-fire of the preceding evening into a blaze. Herman and her sister watched her movements furtively, and saw her change her night-dress, and burn the one she had worn, and which was stained with blood; and as she did so they perceived that her right leg was bleeding profusely, as if from a gun-shot wound. She washed the blood from the white and well-formed limb, and having bandaged it, went into her bedchamber. In a few minutes she came out, dressed, and sat down by the fire, where she remained until Krantz arose.

Astonishment at what they had seen, wonder as to what had become of Hugo, and anxiety as to his fate, kept the children awake until daylight, and when Krantz entered the room, Herman asked, in an hesitating manner, what had become of him.

"Hugo!" said Krantz, glancing towards the bed. "Why were can he be? he must have gone out."

"I thought as I laid awake in the night I heard some one open the outer door," observed Christine. "And where is your gun?' she added looking up to the wall where it usually hung.

Krantz cast his eyes up above the chimney and perceived that his gun was missing. For a moment he looked alarmed and perplexed; then he took a woodman's axe, and left the cottage without speaking another word.

He was not absent long; in a few minutes he returned, bearing in his arms the body of his eldest boy, which was covered with blood and frightfully mangled, as if by the fangs of some savage animal. He laid the corpse upon he floor, and throwing himself upon a seat, covered his face with his hands.

"Merciful heaven!" exclaimed Christine, "what ferocious beast has done this?"

She looked earnestly at the mangled corpse, and Herman and Marcella threw themselves by its side, wailing and sobbing bitterly.

"He must have taken the gun down to shoot a wolf, and the animal has been too powerful for him," continued Christine. "Poor boy! he has paid dearly for his rashness."

Krantz neither spoke nor withdrew his hands from his pale and tearful countenance. Herman wished to speak—to tell all, but Marcella, who perceived his intention, held him by the arm, and looked at him so imploringly, that he desisted. Krantz seemed to accept the explanation of the tragedy which had been suggested by his wife; but the two children, though they could not comprehend it, had a strong impression on their minds that there was some connection between the death of their brother and their step-mother's wounded leg.

In the evening Krantz took a spade, and left the cottage; and at the distance of a few yards, beneath the dusky branches of a huge pine-tree, he hollowed out a grave. With tears coursing each other down his cheeks, he laid within it the mangled remains of his first born child, and when he had filled up the grave, he raised a pile of stones above it, at once to mark the spot, and to prevent the wolves from disinterring the body.

This shocking catastrophe was a severe shock to Krantz, and for several days he never went to the chase, though at times he would utter bitter anathemas and threats of vengeance against the wolves. During this period of mourning on his part, Christine continued her mysterious nocturnal wanderings with the same regularity as before; but still the children refrained from mentioning the subject to their father, fearing that disclosures so strange would be discredited, and have no other result than to bring punishment upon themselves.

At length Krantz took down his gun one morning, and went into the forest; but soon afterwards returned, with signs of grief and vexation on his countenance.

"Would you believe it, Christine?" said he. "The wolves—perdition to the whole race!—have actually contrived to dig up the body of my poor boy, and now there is nothing left of him but the bones."

Christine uttered an expression of surprise, Marcella looked at Herman who read in her intelligent features all she would have said.

"A wolf growls under our window every night, father," observed little Herman.

"Does there?" said Krantz. "Why did you not tell me so before? Wake me the next time you hear it."

Christine glared fiercely on Herman for a moment, and then turned away, the colour fading from her cheeks and lips, though her eyes were lighted up with a lurid blaze. Krantz went out, and re-consigned to the grave the ghastly remains of his son which the wolves had spared, again piling up the stones, as a memorial and a protection.

The spring now came on! the snow disappeared before the warm breath of April, and the trees began to change the russet livery of winter for their more lively garb of green. The violet and the primrose had put forth their modest blossoms on sloping banks, where the sere leaves which the winds of autumn had thickly strewn there had protected them from the frost; and the redbreast, the whitethroat, and the waxwing flew from spray to spray, rejoicing in the change that had come over the face of nature.

The children were now permitted to leave the cottage, but Herman would never quit for one moment the lovely little Marcella, to whom, since the shocking death of their brother, he was more ardently attached than ever. He was afraid, though he scarcely knew why, to leave her alone with their step-mother, who seemed to take an unnatural delight in ill-treating the child. As the spring advanced, Christine's nocturnal rambles in the forest decreased in frequency; and it may be remarked here, that the children never heard the growl of the wolf under the window after Herman had mentioned it to his father.

One day, when Krantz was working on his little farm, and the children were sitting on a bank, beneath the shade of a spreading tree, Herman weaving a garland of wild flowers for his sister, who watched him with infantile delight sparkling in her blue eyes, Christine came towards them, saying that she was going into the forest to collect some herbs, and that Marcella must go to the cottage, and watch the dinner. The child went, and Christine soon disappeared in the forest, taking a direction quite contrary to that in which the cottage stood, and leaving Krantz and the boy, as it were, between her and Marcella.

About an hour afterwards they were startled by shrieks from the cottage, evidently the shrieks of the little Marcella.

"Marcella has burnt herself, father!" exclaimed Herman, starting up, and bounding towards the cottage.

Krantz threw down his spade, and hastened after him. The shrieks had ceased before they could reach the cottage, and when they were within a few yards of it, out darted, through the open door a large white wolf, which fled with the utmost celerity. Krantz had no weapon, an therefore did not pursue the animal; but rushed into the cottage, where the first object that met his horrified gaze was poor little Marcella; lying upon the floor in the agonies of death! Her body and limbs were shockingly torn and lacerated, and she was covered with blood, which also formed a pool upon the cottage floor.

The first intention of the bereaved father had been to seize his gun, and pursue the wolf; but this shocking spectacle stayed his purpose, and he knelt down by the side of his dying child, and burst into tears. Marcella fixed her blue eyes on her father and brother for a moment, and then a shudder pervaded her limbs, and the eyelids closed in death. At that moment Christine came in; she started at the dreadful sight that met her eyes, and expressed much concern but she did not recoil from the sight of the blood so much as most women would have done.

"Poor child!" said she. "It must have been that great white wolf that passed me just now, and frightened me so; she is quite dead, Krantz."

"I know it—I know it!" said he, in a tone of agony.

He mourned bitterly over the body of his sweet child, and seemed as if he would never recover from the shock. He would not allow it to be buried for several days, though frequently requested by his wife to do so. At length he yielded, and dug a grave for it close to that of Hugo, and took every precaution that it should not be disturbed in its last sad resting-place by the ravenous wolves.

Little Herman was now very miserable and sad, for he missed the society of Marcella even more than he had done that of his brother; and he could not help thinking that his step-mother was in some way implicated in both their deaths, although he could not account for the manner: but he no longer felt afraid of Christine, towards whom his little heart was full of hatred and revenge.

The night after Marcella had been buried beneath the pine-tree, by the side of Hugo, Herman perceived his step-mother leave the cottage in her night-dress, as she had so often done. He waited a few minutes, and then rose and dressed himself, determined to follow her, as Hugo had done, whatever might be the consequences. He opened the door, and looked out; the moon was shining brightly, and he could see the spot where his brother and sister were buried. Horror of horrors! he beheld his step-mother kneeling by the side of his sister's grave, from which she was hastily removing the stones which covered it. This done, she began digging and scratching with her hands, throwing the earth behind her with the savage energy of a wild beast. It was some time before the horrified boy could collect his thoughts, and decide what he would do. By the time he had sufficiently recovered from the shock to be able to act, she had arrived at the corpse, and dragged it out of the grave.

"Father! father!" cried the boy, running to the door of the inner chamber. "Dress yourself and get your gun."

"So the wolves are there, are they?" said Krantz, jumping out of bed, and hastily dressing himself.

Without perceiving the absence of his wife, he hurried into the outer room, snatched his gun from the wall, and rushed out, followed by Hermau. To his horror he beheld, as he advanced towards the pine-tree, not a wolf, but his wife, crouching by the body of his dead child, and tearing off large pieces of the flesh which she devoured with the ferocious avidity of a wild beast. She was too busy to be aware of their approach, but Krantz was overpowered for a moment by the fearful shock. He dropped the gun, he breathed heavily, and his hair stood up-right with horror. Herman picked up the gun, and put it in his father's hand. Then he seemed all at once to recover his vigour and presence of mind, aud raising the gun to his shoulder, pulled the trigger. There was a flash and a report, and a loud shriek, down dropped the unnatural monster, in the midst of her horrible banquet.

"God of heaven!" ejaculated the wretched man, as soon as he had discharged the gun, and then he fell down in a swoon.

Herman ran into the cottage for water, which he sprinkled upon his father's face, and in a few minutes restored him to conciousness.

"Where am I?—what has happened?" groaned the wretched man, rolling his eyes about wildly. "Ah, I recollect! Heaven forgive me!"

He rose slowly, and tottered towards the grave; but to the horror and astonishment of both himself and Herman, they beheld, lying over the mangled remains of poor Marcella, not the dead body of Christine, as they expected, but that of a large white wolf.

"The white wolf!" exclaimed Krantz, clasping his hands. "The white she-wolf that lured me into the haunted clearance! I see it all now—I have dealt with the spirits of the Hartz mountains!"

For some minutes the wretched man stood rooted to the spot, in silence and deep thought. He then carefully lifted up the mangled remains of poor Marcella, replaced them in the grave, which he filled up, and covered with stones, as before. Then he struck the head of the dead animal with the heel of his boot, and raving frantically, returned to the cottage. He closed the door, and threw himself upon the bed, groaning and tearing his hair; while Herman sat down in a corner, affrighted and bewildered.

All at once the door of the cottage was thrown violently open, and the hunter Wilford Barnsdorf, rushed in, his swarthy countenance distorted with rage.

"My daughter, man!—my daughter! Where is my daughter?" he exclaimed.

"Where the wretch should be, I trust," returned Krantz starting up, and speaking with equal sternness. "Where she should be—in hell! Leave this cottage, or you may share her fate."

"Ha, ha!" cried the hunter. "Think you to harm a potent spirit of the Hartz mountains? Poor mortal! who would wed a weir-wolf."

"Out, demon!" exclaimed Krantz. "I defy thee and thy power!"

"Yet shall you feel it," rejoined the hunter, with stern emphasis. "Remember your oath—your solemn oath—never to raise your hand against her to harm her."

"I made no compact with evil spirits," said Krantz.

"You did," returned the hunter; "and if you failed in your vow, you were to incur the vengeance of the spirits. Your children were to perish by the vulture and the wolf,"—

"Out, demon! out!" cried Krantz, seizing his axe.

"And their bones to blanch in the wilderness," continued the hunter, unmoved by the wrath of the bereaved father. "Ha, ha, ha!" and he laughed exultingly.

Krantz, frantic with rage, raised his axe to strike, but the hunter moved not an inch; with folded arms he stood, frowning grim defiance upon the excited tenant of the cot.

"All this I swear!" he said, mockingly, while yet the axe gleamed above his head in the pale moonlight.

The axe descended, but it passed through the form of the hunter, and the enfuriated Krantz lost his balance, and fell heavily on the floor.

"Mortal!" said the hunter, in a deep-toned voice, as he strode over the body of his victim, "we have power over those only who had comitted murder. You have been guilty of a double murder, and you shall pay the penalty aattached to your marriage vow. Two of your children are gone—the third is to follow; and follow he will, for your oath is registered. Go—it were kindness to kill thee; four punishment is that you live!"

With these words the demon-hunter disappeared. Krantz rose from the floor, embraced Herman tenderly, and then knelt down to pray.

The next morning he quitted the cottage for ever. Taking Herman with him, he bent his steps towards Holland, where they arrived in safety. He had some money with him; but he had not been many days in Amsterdam, before he was seized with a brain fever, and died raving mad. Herman was received into the asylum for orphans, and afterwards was sent to sea as a cabin boy.

Several years had passed away, and Herman was an able seaman aboard a Dutch East Indiaman, when the vessel to which he belonged was driven ashore on a dark and tempestuous night; and all the efforts of the crew to get her off when day dawned being unsuccessful, it was resolved to abandon her and take to the boats. The land on which the the vessel was aground was a low uninhabited island in the Malaysian archipelago, and the crew thought they should be able to reach Batavia. But on the second the storm came on again with increased fury, and the boats being upset, all hands were engulfed in the briny deep. All perished except Herman and a seaman named Vandervelde, who saved themselves by clinging to one of the capsized boats. For two days they drifted with the current, suffering the intolerable agonies of burning thirst, and exposed to the scorching rays of a vertical sun; and on the third the waves cast them ashore on a small island, the interior of which was rocky and mountainous, descending gradually to low land alternate forest and jungle, which continued to the beach.

Dragging their stiff and weary limbs ashore, they refreshed themselves with the milky juice of the cocoa-nuts, which the forests produced in abundance; and then they sat down on a high point of land, to watch for the passing of some vessel. After watching for some time, they became so sleepy that Herman proposed that they should lie down, but Vandervelde urged the danger they might be exposed to from wild beasts, should there be any on the island, and agreed to watch while Herman slept, as they had no means of making a fire to scare them away. When Herman awoke, after a refreshing sleep of several hours, Vandervelde laid down, but he was less inclined to sleep than his comrade who wiled away the time by relating the strange incidents of his early history, as contained in this narrative.

"I have often asked myself," he said, in conclusion, "whether I am to pay the penalty attached to my father's oath. I do not know malevolent beings of another world are permitted to interfere in the affairs of mortals, but I feel satisfied that, in some way or other, I shall."

Hardly had he uttered these words when there was a tremendous roar—a sound like the rush of air—a cry of agony and terror—and a struggle! Vandervelde shuddered, for he perceived the body of his unfortunate comrade carried off through the jungle by an enormous tiger. He gazed with distended eyeballs; and in a few seconds Herman and the tiger had disappeared!

For more than an hour did Vandervelde remain rooted to the spot, but at length the shades of night set in, and the low growling of the beasts of the forest recalled him to a sense of his own danger. He hurried down to the beach, when he descried a vessel; almost frantic with joy at the sight, and exultation at the hope of a speedy deliverance from the horrors by which he was surrounded; he took of his shirt, and waved it in the air as a signal of distress. For a long period no notice was taken of him and the poor fellow abandonded himself to despair for a time, but recovering at length, he clambered up a tall tree and redoubled his efforts to attract attention. Providence had evidently reserved him for a better fate than had befallen his unhappy and unfortunate friend. His signal was seen and answered, and to his inexpressible joy, a boat put off from the ship—he was taken on board, and released from his perilous situation.

"Poor Krantz!" he murmured, as he thought of the shocking fate of Herman. "The prophecy of his destiny has been fulfilled. *His bones will blanch in the wilderness*, and the demon-hunter and his wolfish daughter are avenged!"

His soliloquy was overheard, for one of the seamen, nudging a messmate to arouse his attention, said:

"Harkee!"

"I do," answered tho other.

"Then listen—

"Ay ay!"

They listened, but Vandevelde having again recovered his self-possession was silent, and spoke no more.

"I'll be hanged if he isn't a rum customer," said the seaman who had first spoken.

"I believe you," said the other.

"Do you think he's right in his head?"

"I doubt it," was the reply.

"Had we not better speak to the captain?" said the first seaman enquiringly.

"Think so," said the other briefly.

The captain was summoned, and the stranger was called before him.

They listened to the man's marvellous tale with wonder and attention, and when he spoke of Herman's most unhappy fate—of the Demon Hunter and his wolfish daughter, the most of them stared aghast with horror.

That his own sufferings had been very acute none could doubt—his hollow eyes—his glaring eyeballs—his quivering tone—all pourtrayed it.

"My benefactors—my friends—my saviours!" he cried in the spontaneous burst of eloquence that sprung from his grateful heart; "I speak the truth—the solemn truth!"

"And I believe it!" said the captain emphatically. "I firmly and most faithfully believe it."

"And so do I," said the sailor who had first spoken.

Time softened down the torrors of their superstitions, but not a man of the crew ever forgot the fate of Herman Krantz.

* * * * * * *

Many such legends as the foregoing are current in the Hartz mountains, and other thinly populated districts of Germany, and also in Bohemia, Hungary and Transylvania. Belief in *lycanthropy*, or the transformation of human beings into wolves, was a very prevalent superstition in those countries throughout the middle ages, and lingered in villages far remote from the progressive tendencies of large towns even down to the beginning of the eighteenth century, just as the belief of witchcraft still lingers in those remote corners of our own country which has not yet been penetrated and opened up by the steam locomotive and the electric telegraph.

The old nursery story of Little Red Riding Hood, the wild romance of Wagner the Wehr-wolf, and many others culled from the wondrous storehouse of German literature, are the offspring of this very remarkable superstition.

The various legendary romances to which these beliefs have given rise, paint a moral by illustrating in the most forcible manner, in an attractive form, the evils that arise from connection with sin in any shape.

Few persons will be found in the present day absolutely credulous enough to place implicit reliance in the old German marvels, but tales of the wild and wonderful, have great attractions in all nations and climes, amongst some of the great family of mankind, and hence the publication in our pages of the present legend.—The Demon Hunter.

Bibliotheca Curiosa.

A

NOCTURNAL EXPEDITION

Round My Room,

BY

XAVIER DE MAISTRE.

TRANSLATED FROM THE FRENCH

BY

EDMUND GOLDSMID, F.R.H.S.
F.S.A. (SCOT.)

PRIVATELY PRINTED, EDINBURGH.

1886

This edition is limited to 275 small-paper copies,

and 75 large-paper copies.

A Nocturnal Expedition Round My Room.

I. TO arouse some interest in the new room in which I have performed a Nocturnal Expedition, I must inform the reader how it had fallen to my share. Having my attention continually called away from my work in the noisy house in which I lived, I had long thought of taking a quieter residence, when, one day, reading a biographical notice of Buffon, I found that that celebrated man had chosen in his garden, a lovely summer house, containing only his arm chair and the desk at which he wrote, while the only book admitted was the MS. on which he was engaged.

The trifles which occupy me are so essentially different from the immortal works of Buffon, that the thought of imitating him, even on this point, would certainly not have occurred to me, had it not been for an accident. A servant, dusting the furniture, thought he saw a good deal of dust on a crayon drawing which I had just completed, and wiped it so thoroughly with a cloth that he succeeded in ridding it of all that I had so carefully put into it. After having raved against this fellow, who happened to be out, and after having said nothing to him when he came back, according to my custom, I started off at once and returned with the key of a little room which I had hired on the fifth story of a house in Providence Street. That same day, I had the materials for my favorite employments carried over, and henceforth I spent most of my time there, where domestics ceased to trouble, and picture-cleaners were at rest. Hours passed like minutes, and more than once my reveries caused me to forget the dinner hour.

Sweet Solitude! I have known the charms with which thou dost intoxicate thy lovers. Woe to him who cannot be alone for one day without feeling the weariness of *ennui*, and prefers, if need be, to hold conversation with fools, rather than with himself!

I will confess, however, that I love solitude in large cities; but, unless I am compelled by serious causes, such as "A journey round my room," I do not care to be a hermit except in the morning; in the evening, I like to see human faces again.

The inconveniences of social life, and those of solitude, thus counteract each other, and these two modes of existence thus beautify one another.

The inconstancy and fatality of earthly affairs are such, however, that the vividness of the pleasures that I enjoyed in my new residence ought to have warned me of their probably short duration. The French Revolution, which was surging on all sides, had just overtopped the Alps, and was pouring down upon Italy. The first wave carried me to Bologna. Here, nevertheless, I still kept on my hermitage, into which I had all my furniture moved, to await happier times. For some years I had been an exile: one fine morning I found myself without employment. After a whole year spent in seeing men and things I cared little for, and in wishing for things and men I could no longer see, I returned to Turin. It was necessary to take some definite step. I walked out from the *Hotel de la Bonne Femme*, where I had put up, with the intention of giving up my little room, and selling my furniture.

On re-entering my hermitage, I experienced sensations difficult to describe: Everything was in the same order, I mean the same disorder in which I had left it: The furniture piled up against the wall had been protected from the pust by the lowness of the roof; my pens were still standing in the dried up inkstand, and I found on the table a letter which I had begun.

"I am still at home," I said to myself, with genuine satisfaction.

Each object recalled some event in my life, and my room seemed papered with memories. Instead of returning to the inn, I resolved to spend the night in the midst of my goods and chattels. I sent for my portmanteau, and determindd to start on the morrow, without taking leave or advice from anyone, casting myself without reserve into the hands of Providence.

II. WHILST I was thus reflecting, glorying in this well-defined plan of travel, time was passing, and my servant did not return. He was a man whom necessity had made me take into my service a few weeks before, and as to whose faithfulness I had conceived some suspicions. No sooner did the idea occur to me that he might have carried off my portmanteau, than I ran to the inn: it was quite time. As I turned the corner of the street in which the Hotel de la Bonne Femme is situated, I saw him issue hurriedly from the gateway, following a porter who carried my portmanteau. He had himself undertaken to carry my cash box; and, instead of turning in my direction, he moved off to the left towards a point of the compass opposite to that he ought to have sought. His intention was clear. I easily caught him up, and without saying anything to him, I walked for some time by his side without his perceiving me. Had any one wished to depict the highest degree of astonishment and fear on the human face, he would have made a perfect model, when he saw me at his side. I had plenty of time to study him, for he was so disconcerted by my unexpected apparition and the serious expression of my face as I gazed on him, that he continued the walk on for some time with me without uttering a word, as if we had been taking a walk together. At length he muttered some excuse about some business in the Rue Grand-Doire; but I set him on the right track, and we returned home, when I dismissed him.

It was then only that I determined to make a new journey in my room, during the last night I was to spend in it, and I set about my preparations at once.

III. I HAD long wished to revisit the country which I had formerly so delightfully travelled through, and the description of which did not appear to me to be complete. Some friends who had liked it urged me to continue, and, no doubt, I should have made up my mind to do so sooner, had I not been separated from my travelling companions. Sorrowfully, I again took up my parable. Alas! I took it up alone. I was about to journey, unaccompanied by my dear Joanetti and my amiable Rosine. My first room itself had undergone a most disastrous revolution; nay, it no longer existed. Its walls now formed part of a horrible building blackened by flames, and all the murderous inventions of war had united to destroy it utterly.[1] The wall where hung the portrait of Madame de Hautcastel had been pierced by a shell. In a word, had I not performed my journey before this catastrophe, the learned men of to-day would have had no knowledge of this remarkable chamber. In a similar way, were it not for the observations of Hipparcus, they would be ignorant that there was formerly one star more in the Pleiades, which has disappeared since the days of that famous astronomer.

Already, driven by circumstances, I had forsaken my room some time previously, and transported my Penates elsewhere. No great misfortune, you will say. Yes, but how am I to replace Joanetti and Rosine? Ah! that is impossible. Joanetti had become so necessary to me that I shall never be able to replace him. Who, however, can flatter himself with the hope that he will ever be able to live with those he loves? Like those swarms of

---

[1] De Maistre's former room was situated in the citadel of Turin, which had been taken by the Austro-Prussian army.

flies one sees hovering in the air on fine summer nights, men meet by chance, and for a moment only. Happy if, in their rapid flight, skilful as flies, they do not run their heads against one another!

I was going to bed one night. Joanetti was waiting on me with his usual attention, and appeared even extra zealous. When he took away the light I cast my eyes on him, and I saw a distinct change in his physiognomy. Was I to believe that poor Joanetti was waiting on me for the last time? I will not keep the reader in a state of uncertainty more painful than the truth. I prefer to say at once that Joanetti married that same night and left me the next day.

Let no one, however, accuse him of ingratitude for having left his master so hurriedly. I had known his intention for a long time, and I had been wrong in opposing it. A busybody came to me very early in the morning to give me this information, and I had plenty of time, before seeing Joanetti, to get in a rage and out again, so that he escaped the reproaches he expected. Before entering my room, he pretended to speak loudly to some one in the passage, to make me believe he was not afraid; and, calling to his aid all the brazen-facedness a simple soul like his was capable of, he presented himself with a determined countenance. I saw at once from his face what was passing within him, and I was rather pleased than otherwise. Modern jokers have in our day so frightened people with the danger of marriage, that a bridegroom often resembles a man who has had a frightful fall without hurting himself, and who is at the same time full of fear and delight, which makes him look ridiculous. It was therefore not astonishing if the actions of my faithful servant were influenced by the peculiarity of his situation.

"So you are married, my dear Joanetti," said I, laughing. He had only armed himself against my anger, so that all his precautions were in vain. He fell back at once to his ordinary level, and even a little lower, for he began to shed tears. "What would you have, Sir," replied he, sobbing; "I had given my word."—"Oh! you have done quite right, my friend; may you be satisfied with your wife, and especially with yourself! May you have children like you! We must part, then!"—"Yes, Sir; we are thinking of settling at Asti."—"And when do you want to leave me?" Here Joanetti looked at his feet with an embarrassed air, and answered fully two tones lower: "My wife has found a carrier from her district who is returning empty, and leaves to-day. It would be a fine opportunity; but . . . . nevertheless . . . . it is as you like, Sir, ... although such an opportunity will not be easily found again."—"What! so soon!" said I. A feeling of regret and of affection, mingled with a large dose of irritation, kept me silent for a moment. "No, certainly," replied I, somewhat sharply, "I will not detain you; start at once, if it suits you." Joanetti looked pale. "Yes, go, my friend. Go to your wife. Be always as good, as honest as you have been with me." We settled some small matters; I sadly bade him adieu: he went out.

This man had served me fifteen years. One moment separated us. I have never seen him again.

I was thinking over this sudden parting, as I walked about my room. Rosine had followed Joanetti without his perceiving it. A quarter of an hour later, a door opened; Rosine entered. I saw Joanetti's hand as he pushed her into the room; the door closed, and I felt a pang in my heart: he no longer enters my room! A few minutes have been sufficient to make strangers of two old comrades of fifteen years' standing. Oh, sad, sad condition of humanity! There is not a single stabie object on which man can fix the least of his affections!

IV. ROSINE also was living far away from me. You will perhaps learn with some interest, my dear Mary, that at the age of 15 she was still the most amiable of animals, and the same superior intelligence which formerly distinguished her from all her species now enabled her to bear with resignation the weight of many years. My wish would have been to have kept her; but when the fate of our friends is at stake, ought one only to consult one's pleasure or one's interest? It was necessary that Rosine should give up the perambulating existence she led with me, and enjoy in her latter days a rest her master no longer hoped for. Her age compelled me to have her carried about. I felt it my duty to pension her off. A beneficent nun undertook her care, and I know that in her retreat she enjoyed all the advantages which her good qualities, her age, and her reputation had so deservedly merited.

And since the nature of man is such that it would seem as if happiness were not made for him, since friend unwittingly offends friend, and lovers themselves cannot live without quarreling; since, in a word, from the days of Lycurgus to our own, every legislator has failed in his efforts to make men happy, I, at least, shall have the consolation of having insured the happiness of a dog.

V. NOW that I have acquainted the reader with the last events in the history of Joanetti Rosine, I need only say a word of *Anima* and

Bestia to set myself square with him. These two individuals, especially the latter, will no longer play so interesting a part in my journey. An amiable traveller, who has followed the same itinerary as myself,[1] says they must be tired. Alas ! his observation is but too true. It is not that my soul has lost any of its activity, so far at any rate as I can make out, but her connection with *the other* has altered. Bestia no longer shows the same vivaeity in her retorts ; she no longer has . . . How shall I express it ! . . . I was about to say the same presence of mind, as if mere matter could have any ! However that may be, and without entering into an embarrassing explanation, I will only say that, carried away by the confidence young Alexandrine had shewn me, I wrote her a somewhat tender epistle, to which I received a cool though polite reply, ending in these words : " Be assured, Sir, that I will ever look upon you with feelings of sincerest esteem." Good Heavens ! cried I, I am lost ! Since that fatal day, I resolved no longer to put forward my system of *Anima* and *Bestia.* I shall therefore, without making any distinction between these two beings, and without separating them, push them forward, *unus super alterum*, like merchants do with their merchandise, and I will

[1] The author here alludes to " un second voyage autour de ma chambre," by an anonymous writer.

advance in close formation to avoid any inconvenience.[1]

VI. I NEED not speak of the size of my new room. It is so like my old one, that at first sight you might take it for it, had not the architect taken the precaution to incline the roof, on the side overlooking the street, to the angle required by the laws of hydraulics to enable the rain to fall off. Daylight penetrates through a single opening two and a half feet wide by four feet high, about six or seven feet above the floor, and reached by means of a short ladder.

The elevation of my window above the floor was one of those happy circumstances which may be equally due to chance or to the genius of the architect. The almost perpendicular light thrown into my cell gave it a mysterious aspect. The ancient Temple of the Pantheon receives its light in almost the same way. Besides this, no exterior object could distract my attention. Like those navigators lost on the vasty deep, who see but sky and water, I could see but the sky and my room, and the nearest exterior objects that met my eyes were the moon or the morning star; which fact placed me in immediate connection with heaven, and gave to my thoughts an elevated

[1] To understand this chapter the reader should be acquainted with De Maistre's "Journey Round my Room."

tendency they would never have had, had I chosen to lodge on the first floor.

The window I am speaking of looked out over the roof, and formed the prettiest frame to the landscape. Its elevation was such that when the rays of the rising sun first lighted it, it was still dark in the street. The view was one of the finest that can be imagined. But the loveliest view becomes monotonous when too often seen; the eye becomes accustomed to it, and it is no longer made much of. The position of my window enabled me to avoid this inconvenience, for, as I never saw the magnificent spectacle of the environs of Turin without climbing four or five steps, my enjoyment was always keen because not too often indulged in. When, weary, I wished for some agreeable recreation, I closed my day by climbing up to my window.

On the first step I saw nothing but the sky; soon, the colossal temple of Superga[1] began to appear. The hill on which Turin rests, rose gradually before me, covered with woods and rich vineyards, spreading forth with pride before the setting sun its gardens and its palaces, whilst simple and modest dwellings seemed to half hide

---

[1] A magnificent church built by Victor Amadeus I. in 1706 in accomplishment of a vow to the Virgin in the event of the French raising the siege of Turin. It is the burial place of the princes of the house of Savoy.

themselves in its valleys, offering retreats to the wise and favoring their meditations.

Charming hill! often hast thou seen me seek thy solitary nooks, and prefer thine unfrequented paths to the brilliant promenades of the capital; often hast thou seen me lost in thy labyrinths of verdure, listening to the morning song of the lark, my heart full of a vague unrest, and longing earnestly to spend my life in thine enchanting valleys. Hail to thee, charming hill! thou art imprinted on my heart. May the dew of Heaven, if it be possible, render thy fields more fertile, and thy groves more shady! May thine inhabitants enjoy their happiness in peace, and thy leafy bowers ensure perfect rest! May thy fruitful soil ever be the sweet refuge of true philosophy, of modest science, and of the sincere and hospitable friendship that welcomed me when there!

VII. I BEGAN my journey punctually at eight o'clock in the Evening, the weather was calm and promised a fine night. I had taken my precautions to be alone till midnight, and not to be disturbed by visitors, who are scarce at the height where I dwelt, and especially under the circumstances in which I found myself. Four hours would be quite sufficient for the execution of the enterprise, as I only intended to make a short excursion round my room. If my first journey lasted 42 days, that was because I was unable to shorten it. I did not intend to travel in a carriage as before, feeling sure that a pedestrian sees much that is missed by him who takes post horses. I therefore resolved to travel alternately, or according to circumstances, on foot or on horseback: a new method which I have not yet made known, and whose usefulness will be soon seen. Lastly, I determined to take notes on the road, and to write down my observations as they occurred to me, so as not to forget anything.

In order to carry out my plan systematically, and to give it a further chance of success, I thought I ought to begin with a dedication, written in verse, to make it more interesting. But two difficulties occurred to me and nearly made me give up the idea, notwithstanding its apparent advantages. The first was to know to whom to address the dedication, and the second was how to make verses. After having thought it well over, I saw that reason demanded that I should write my dedication first and then consider to whom it was best suited. I set to work at once and laboured for more than an hour to find a rhyme to the first line I had written, and which I wished to preserve, as it seemed to me rather good. I then luckily remembered that I had read somewhere that Pope never composed anything interesting save after repeating many lines aloud and moving rapidly about his study to excite his energy. I at once tried to imitate him. I took the poems of Ossian and repeated them aloud, pacing my room to arouse my enthusiasm.

I perceived that this method certainly warmed my imagination, and gave me a secret feeling of poetic capacity, which I should have made use of to compose successfully my dedication in verse, had I not unfortunately forgotten the obliquity of the roof of my room, whose acute angle prevented my forehead from going as far as my feet in the direction I had taken. I struck so hard against this confounded wall, that the roof of the house was shaken: the sparrows that slept under the eaves fled, filled with terror, and the concussion sent me fully three steps back.

VIII. WHILST I was thus walking about to excite my imagination, a young and pretty woman who lodged below, astonished at the noise I was making, and thinking, perhaps, I was giving a dance in my room, despatched her husband to find out the reason of the disturbance. I was still confused with the blow I had experienced when the door opened. An elderly man, with a melancholy face, put in his head, and gave an inquisitive glance round the room. When the surprise of finding me alone allowed him to speak, he said, "My wife has a headache,

Sir. Allow me to call your attention . . . ." I interrupted him at once, and my style reflected the height my thoughts had risen to. "Respectable messenger of my lovely neighbour," said I in the language of the bards, "why do thine eyes sparkle beneath thy bushy eyebrows, like two meteors in the black forest of Cromba? Thy lovely mate is a ray of light, and I would die a thousand deaths ere I troubled her repose; but thine aspect, oh respectable messenger, thine aspect is dark as the furthermost vault of the Cavern of Camora, when the gathered storm-clouds darken the face of night, and lower over the silent plains of Morven."

The neighbour, who had apparently never read the poems of Ossian, foolishly mistook this fit of enthusiasm for a fit of lunacy, and seemed much embarrassed. Having no intention to offend him, I offered him a chair, and begged him to be seated; but I perceived that he softly withdrew, making the sign of the Cross, and murmuring: "E matto, per Baccho, è matto!"[1]

IX. I LET him go out without caring to enquire how far his observation was correct, and I sat down to my desk to take note of these events

---

[1] "He's mad, by Jove, mad."

as usual; but hardly had I opened a drawer where I expected to find some paper, than I hastily closed it, filled with one of the most disagreeable sensations one can experience, that of humbled pride. The species of surprise with which I was filled on that occasion resembles that experienced by a thirsty traveller when, putting his lips to a limpid stream, he perceives, at the bottom, a frog looking at him. It was nothing more, however, than the springs and carcase of an artificial dove, which, following the example of Archytas, I had formerly endeavoured to make. I had worked unceasingly at its construction for more than three months. The day of trial having come, I placed it at the edge of a table, after having carefully closed the door, so as to keep my discovery a secret, and cause pleasant surprise to my friends. A thread kept the mechanism immovable. Who can imagine the palpitations of my heart, and my feeling of anxiety as I seized the scissors to cut the fateful thread? . . . . There! . . . . The spring in the dove starts and begins noisily to work. I raise my eyes to see it pass; but after one or two turns, it falls and hides itself under the table. Rosine, who was sleeping there, sadly walked away. Rosine, who never yet saw a fowl, or pigeon, or the smallest bird without attacking it and pursuing it, did not even deign to look at my dove struggling on the floor. This was the last stab given to my pride. I went out for a walk on the ramparts.

X. SUCH was the fate of my artificial dove. Whilst my mechanical genius destined it to follow the eagle into the skies, fate gave it the instincts of a mole.

I was walking about sad and discouraged, as is natural after a great hope disappointed, when, raising my eyes, I perceived a flock of wild geese, passing over my head. I stopped to watch them. They advanced in triangular formation, like the English column at the battle of Fontenoy. I saw them speed from cloud to cloud. "Ah! how well they fly, murmured I; with what assurance they glide along the invisible path they are following." Shall I confess it! alas! may I be forgiven! the horrible feeling of envy once, once only, entered my heart, and I was envious of geese. I followed them with jealous eyes to the limit of the horizon. Long, motionless amidst the crowd of loungers, I watched the rapid flight of the swallows, and I was surprised at seeing them suspended in mid air, as if I had never observed this phenomenon before. A feeling of profound admiration, unknown before, filled my heart. I listened with astonishment to the buzzing of the insects, to the song of the birds, and to that mysterious and confused sound of all living creation unwittingly celebrating its author. Inexpressible concert, wherein man alone has the sublime privilege of uttering hymns of thanksgiving! "Who is the author of this brilliant mechanism? Who is he who, opening his creative hand, sent out the first swallow to fly in the air? Who is he who ordered the trees to spring from the ground and raise their branches towards the sky? And thou, that majestically walkest under their shade, enchanting creature whose features command respect and love, who has placed thee on the surface of the earth to embellish it? What mind designed thy divine form, and created the look and smile of innocent beauty? And I, myself, who feel my heart beat, what is the object of my existence? Who am I, and whence come I, I, the author of the centripetal artificial dove?" Hardly had I pronounced this barbarous name than, recovering my senses suddenly like a sleeper o'er whom a pail of cold water has been thrown, I perceived that several persons were surrounding me and examining me, whilst my enthusiasm led me to talk aloud. I then saw lovely Georgina walking a few paces ahead of me. Half her left cheek, loaded with rouge, peeping through the curls of her golden wig, placed me once again on a level with the things of this world, from which I had made a short excursion.

XI. AS soon as I had somewhat recovered from the shock which the sight of my artificial dove had caused me, the pain of the blow I had received made itself keenly felt. I put my hand to my forehead and found a new bump just where Dr. Gall has placed the bump of poetry. But I did not think of that then, and experience alone was to demonstrate to me the truth of that celebrated man's system.

After having collected my thoughts for a moment before making a last effort at my dedication, I took a pencil and set to work. Conceive my astonishment! Lines appeared to spring from the paper; I filled two pages in less than one hour, and I concluded from this circumstance that, if movement was necessary for Pope's head to compose verses, nothing less than a blow could get them out of mine. I will, however, not give the reader those that I then composed, for the prodigious rapidity with which the adventures of my journey followed one another, prevented my putting a finishing touch to them. Notwithstanding this reticence on my part, the accident which had happened to me must be looked upon as a precious discovery, of which poets cannot make too much use.

I am indeed so convinced of the infallibility of this new method, that, in the poem in four and twenty cantos which I have since then composed, and which will be published with "The Prisoner of Pignerol,"[1] I have not thought it necessary as yet to begin the verses; but I have neatly copied out 500 pages of notes, which form, as every one knows, the whole merit and the greater part of the bulk of most modern poems.

As I was thinking deeply over my discoveries and walking about my room, I came across my bed, on which I sat down, and my hand falling by chance on my nightcap, I made up my mind to cover my head with it and go to bed.

XII. I HAD been in bed about a quarter of an hour and, as usual, I was not yet asleep. The saddest reflections had succeeded the thought of my dedication: my candle, drawing to an end, cast a fitful and solemn light, and my room had the appearance of a tomb. A gust of wind suddenly blew the window open, extinguished my candle, and banged the door. The dark hue of my thoughts was increased by the darkness.

All my past pleasures, all my present troubles, fell on my heart and filled it with regrets and bitterness.

Although I make continual efforts to forget my griefs and drive them from my thoughts, it some-

---

[1] Both poem and romance are fictitious.

times happens, when not on the watch, that they suddenly re-enter my memory in a body, as if a dam had given way. There is nothing for me then but to yield to the torrent, and my thoughts then become so black, everything seems to me so dark, that I generally end by laughing at my folly; thus the violence of the evil brings with it its own remedy.

I was still in the midst of one of these melancholy fits, when a part of the gust, which had opened my window and closed my door on its passage, after taking a turn or two in my room, turned the leaves of my books, and throwing a loose sheet of my travels to the ground, finally entered my curtains and died on my cheek. I felt the sweet freshness of the night, and considering it an invitation on its part, I arose at once, and climbed my ladder to enjoy the calm of nature.

XIII. THE weather was fine: the milky way, like a slight cloud, divided the sky; a gentle ray of light fell on me from each star, and when I watched one attentively, its companions seemed to twinkle more vividly to attract my eyes, and these thoughts passed through my mind:—

It is ever for me a fresh enjoyment to contemplate the starry heavens, and I cannot reproach myself with having accomplished a single journey, or even a mere evening walk, without paying the tribute of admiration I owe to the marvels of the firmament. Although I feel the full want of power of my meditations, I find in them an inexpressible pleasure. I love to imagine that it is not chance that carries to my eyes the light that emanates from these far off worlds, and each star sheds with its light a ray of hope into my heart. What! shall these marvels have no other connection with me than that of merely shining before my eyes? And my thought, that rises to their level, my heart, which vibrates at their aspect, shall they be strangers to them? Ephemeral spectator of an eternal spectacle, man raises for a second his eyes to Heaven, and closes them for ever; but, during that rapid second that is granted to him, from all the quarters of Heaven, and from the outer limits of the Universe, a consoling ray darts from each world and meets his eyes, to announce to him that some connection exists between him and infinity, and that even he is linked to eternity.

XIV. ONE unpleasant feeling grated however on the pleasure I experienced in these meditations:—

How few people, I thought to myself, are now enjoying with me the sublime spectacle which Heaven spreads in vain before weary humanity! It may be all very well for those who are asleep; but what would it cost those who are walking abroad, those who are crowding out of the theatres, to look for one moment with admiration on the brilliant constellations that shine everywhere above their heads? No; the attentive spectators of Scapin and of Jocrisse[1] will not deign to raise their eyes; they will brutally return to their homes, or elsewhere, without dreaming that the sky exists. How curious it is! because one can see it often, and for nothing, they will have none of it. If the heavens were always hidden from us, if the view it offers depended on a lessee, the stage boxes on the roofs of the houses would fetch fabulous prices, and the ladies of Turin would tear their eyes out to obtain my attic window. "Oh, were I but sovereign of some country! cried I, filled with just indignation, I would have the alarm bell rung each night, and I would force my subjects of every age, of every sex, and of every condition, to look out of the window and gaze on the stars." Here Reason, who in my kingdom has only a limited right of remonstrance, was happier than usual in her objections on the subject of the inconsiderate decree I was thinking of issuing in my States. "Sire," said she, "would not your Majesty deign to make an exception in favour of rainy nights, for, in that case, the sky being cloudy, ..." "Quite right, quite right, I had not thought of that: you may note an exception in favour of rainy nights." "Sire, I think it might be well to except also those fine nights when cold is excessive, or when the north wind blows, for the rigorous execution

[1] Two comic characters in Moliere's plays.

of your decree would overwhelm your happy subjects with colds and catarrhs." I began to see a good many difficulties in the way of executing my projects; but I did not like to change my mind. "You will have to write," said I, "to the Council of Medicine, and to the Academy of Sciences, in order to fix what degree of the Centigrade thermometer will excuse my subjects from going to the window; but I require, I insist, that my orders shall be carried out rigorously." "And the sick, sire?" "Of course, let them be excepted: Humanity must be first considered." "If I were not afraid of fatiguing your Majesty, I would suggest that one might (in case your Majesty thought it right, and no great inconvenience be experienced) make another exception in favour of the blind, since, being deprived of the organ of sight, ..." "Well, is that all?" I inquired, with irritation. "Pardon me, Sire; but lovers? The kind heart of your Majesty would not constrain lovers to gaze at the stars?" "Very well, very well," said the King, "we will put it off for the present; we will take time to think of it. You had better give me a detailed report on the matter."

Good Heavens! how one must reflect before issuing a mere police regulation!

XV. THE most brilliant stars have never been those which have caused me the most pleasure; but the smallest, those which, lost in immeasurable space, appear mere imperceptible specks, have always been my favourities. The reason is simple: You will easily understand that, causing my imagination to travel as far beyond their sphere as my eyes do to reach to them, I find myself transported without an effort to a distance such as few travellers have covered before me, and I am astonished, when reaching that point, to find myself only at the beginning of this vast Universe; for it would, I think, be ridiculous to imagine that there exists a barrier beyond which chaos begins, as if chaos were easier to comprehend than existence! Beyond the last star I picture to myself another, which itself cannot be the last. By assigning limits, however remote, to creation, the Universe appears to me but a luminous speck, compared to the immensity of emptiness which surrounds it with that fearful and gloomy chaos, in the midst of which it would be suspended like a solitary lamp. Here I covered my eyes with my two hands, to concentrate my thoughts, and give to my ideas the depth required by such a subject; and, making a supreme effort, I composed a system of the world, the most complete that has yet appeared. Here it is in all its details; it is the result of the meditations of my whole life: *I believe that space being* . . . . but this deserves a separate chapter; and, considering the importance of the matter, it shall be the only one in the narrative of my journey which shall have a title.

CHAPTER XVI.

SYSTEM OF THE WORLD.

I BELIEVE, then, that space being infinite, creation is infinite also, and that God, during his Eternity, has created an infinitude of worlds in the immensity of space.

XVII. I WILL, however, confess in good faith that I hardly understood my own system better than all the other systems produced up to this day by the imagination of ancient and modern philosophers; but mine has the precious advantage of being contained in four lines, enormous though it be. The indulgent reader will please to observe, also, that it has been entirely composed at the top of a ladder. I should, however, have embellished it with commentaries and notes if, at the moment when I was most occupied with my subject, I had not been disturbed by certain enchanting sounds which agreeably met my ear. A voice, the most melodious I have ever heard, not even excepting that of Zeneida—one of those voices which are always in unison with the strings of my heart—sang, close to me, a ballad of which I did not miss one word, and which shall ever remain in my memory. Listening attentively, I found that the voice issued from a window lower than mine; unfortunately, I could not see it, the ledge of the roof, above which was my attic window, hiding it from my eyes.

The desire to catch sight of the siren who charmed me by her melody increased as the words of the ballad brought tears into my eyes. Soon, unable to resist my curiosity longer, I climbed to the top of the ladder, placed a foot on the edge of the roof, and, holding on to the framework of the window with one hand, I overhung the street, at the risk of breaking my neck.

I then saw on a balcony to my left, somewhat below me, a young woman in a white dressing-gown: her head rested on her hand, and was sufficiently bent to enable me to catch a glance, with the aid of the starlight, of a most interesting profile. Her attitude seemed purposely intended to give an aeriel traveller like myself the best view of a small yet well-developed figure; one of her naked feet, thrown slightly back, was so placed that notwithstanding the darkness I could make out its small size, whilst a pretty little slipper, apart from it, certified it still better to my curious eyes. I leave you to imagine, my dear Sophia, the awkwardness of my position. I did not dare utter the slightest exclamation, for fear of startling my pretty neighbour, nor to make the least movement, for fear of falling into the street. A sigh, however, escaped me; but I was in time to keep back half of it; the remainder was carried away by a zephyr which happened to pass by; and I had plenty of leisure to examine the fair dreamer, sustained in my perilous position by the hope of hearing her sing again. But, alas! her ballad was done, and my evil genius led her to maintain a most obstinate silence. At length, after having waited long, I thought I might venture to speak to her: I had only to find some compliment worthy of her and of the feelings she had inspired me with. Oh! how much I regretted not having completed my dedication in verse! What an excellent opportunity I should have had of making use of it! My presence of mind did not fail me in my need. Inspired by the soft influence of the stars, and by the still more powerful wish to make an impression on this lovely woman—after having gently coughed, to warn her and to soften the sound of my voice—in the most affectionate manner I remarked: "It is very fine to night."

XVIII. I THINK I hear Madame de Haut-Castel, who never lets me off anything, asking me for particulars of the ballad I mentioned in the preceding chapter. For the first time in my life, I find myself under the painful necessity of refusing her something. If I inserted these lines in my voyage, I should be undoubtedly considered the author of them, which would draw upon me, on the subject of blows on the head, many a jest I prefer avoiding. I shall therefore continue to relate my adventure with my amicable neighbour, an adventure the unexpected catastrophe of which, and the delicacy I showed therein, are well fitted to interest all classes of readers. But, before telling what her answer was, and how she received the ingenious compliment I had paid her, I must reply to certain persons who think themselves more eloquent than I was, and who will condemn me without mercy for having commenced a conversation in a manner so trivial, at any rate in their opinion. I will prove to them that, had I been witty on that important occasion, I should have openly transgressed the rules of prudence and good taste. Any man, who enters into conversation with a woman, either with an epigram or a compliment, however flattering, discovers pretensions which should only appear when they begin to have a foundation. Besides, if he tries wit, it is clear that he seeks to shine, and, consequently, that he is thinking less of the lady than of himself. Now, ladies like to be thought of; and although they have not always the precise thoughts I have written down, they possess a delicate and natural instinct which tells them that a trivial phrase, spoken simply to enter into conversation and approach them, is worth a thousand witticisms inspired by vanity, or even (which will appear astonishing) than a dedication in verse. Moreover I maintain (though my opinion may be considered a paradox), that light and brilliant wit in conversation is not even necessary during the longest courtship, if the heart has really called it into existence; and, notwithstanding everything that is said by persons who have only half loved of the long intervals that separate the paroxisms of love or friendship, time is always too short when spent with one's love, and silence is as interesting as discussion.

. . . .

However that may be, it is quite certain that I found nothing better to say from the edge of the roof where I was, than the words in question. I had hardly uttered them, before my soul was transported to the drum of my ears, to catch the faintest echo of the sounds I hoped to hear. The lovely creature raised her head to look at me: her long hair spread round her like a veil, and acted as a background to her charming face, wherein was reflected the mysterious light of the stars. Already her lips separated to utter sweet words . . . . but, oh Heavens! what was my surprise and my terror! a sinister noise resounded and a masculine and sonorous voice from the interior of the apartment, exclaimed: "What are you doing there, Madam, at this hour? Come in!" I was petrified.

XIX. SUCH must be the sound which terrifies the guilty when the burning gates of Tartarus are suddenly opened before them; or that caused beneath the infernal vaults by the seven cataracts of the Styx, which the poets have forgotten to mention.

XX. A SHOOTING star crossed the sky at this moment, and disappeared almost at once. My eyes, which the brilliancy of the meteor had attracted for a moment, returned to the balcony, and saw nothing there but the little slipper. My neighbour, in her hurried flight, had forgotten to pick it up. I gazed long at this pretty cast of a foot worthy of Praxiteles with an emotion I dare not confess the extent of, but what will appear very singular, and I cannot explain it to myself, is that an overpowering attraction prevented my removing my eyes from it, in spite of every effort to direct them to some other object.

It is said that when a serpent looks at a nightingale, the unfortunate bird, the victim of an irresistible spell, is forced to approach the voracious reptile. Its rapid wings only lead it to its ruin, and every effort to get away only brings it nearer to the enemy, which follows it with its eyes. Such was the effect on me of this slipper, without, however, my being able to say with certainty which of us two, the slipper and I, was the serpent, since, according to the laws of physic, the attraction should have been reciprocal. It is certain that this fatal influence was not a play of my imagination. I was really so strongly attracted, that I was twice on the point of letting go and of falling. Nevertheless, as the balcony I wished to reach was not exactly under my window, but a little to the side, I saw very clearly that the force of gravitation invented by Newton, combining itself with the oblique attraction of the slipper, I should have followed in my fall a diagonal line, and I should have fallen on a sentry box, which, from the height I was at, looked no bigger than an egg, so that my object would not have been attained. . . . I therefore clutched my window the more firmly, and, making a supreme effort, I managed to raise my eyes and to look at the sky.

XXI. I SHOULD find it very difficult to explain and define correctly the kind of pleasure I felt on this occasion. All I can affirm is that it was quite unlike that which, a few moments before, the sight of the milky way and the starry sky had caused me. Yet, as in the most embarassing situations of life I have always tried to understand what was passing in my soul, I endeavoured now to ascertain exactly what pleasure an honest man can find in watching a lady's slipper, as compared with that caused by the contemplation of the stars. With this object I picked out in the sky the most brilliant constellation. It was, I believe, Cassiopœa's Chair which was above my head, and I looked from the constellation to the slipper, and from the slipper to the constellation. I then found that these two sensations were of an entirely different character: One was in my head, whilst the other seemed to affect my heart. But what I cannot confess without some shame is that the attraction of the enchanted slipper absorbed all my faculties. The enthusiasm which, a few moments before, the sight of the stars had caused me only existed now in a feeble degree, and soon it vanished utterly when I heard the window on the balcony open, and perceived a little foot, whiter than alabaster, advancing softly to seize the little slipper. I tried to speak; but, not having had time to prepare myself as on the first occasion, I no longer found my usual presence of mind, and I heard the window close before I had thought of anything suitable to say.

XXII. THE foregoing chapters will suffice, I hope, to answer victoriously an accusation of Madame de Hautcastel's, who has not hesitated to attack my first Journey, under the pretext that one has no opportunity of making love in it. She could not say the same of my new journey; and, although my adventure with my amiable neighbour was not pushed very far, I affirm I found more satisfaction in it than in many others, wherein I had considered myself very fortunate, for want of some object of comparison. Every one enjoys life in his own way; but I should not think I had treated my benevolent reader well, were I to hide from him a discovery which, more than anything else, has contributed to my happiness (on condition, however, of its remaining a secret between us). It is nothing less than a new system of love-making, far more advantageous than the old one, without any of its numerous inconveniences. This invention being specially adapted for persons who may adopt my new mode of travelling, I consider I ought to devote a few chapters to their instruction.

XXIII. I HAD observed in the course of my life that, when I was in love according to the usual plan, my sensations never equalled my hopes, and my imagination was defeated in all its projects. On thinking the matter over carefully, it struck me that if I could extend the feeling which inclines me to the love of an individual to the whole sex, I might secure new enjoyments without compromising myself in any way. What could be said, in fact, to a man with a heart capable of loving all the amiable women of the universe? Yes, Madam, I love them all, and not only those I know or expect to meet with, but all those that exist on the surface of the earth; much more: I love every woman that has ever existed, and those that will hereafter exist, without counting a much larger number whom my imagination creates: every possible woman, in a word, is comprised in the vast circle of my affections.

By what unjust and strange caprice should I enclose a heart like mine within the narrow limits of one society? Nay, why circumscribe its flight within the limits of one kingdom or even of one republic?

Seated at the foot of an oak, beaten by the storm, a young Indian widow mingles her sighs with the roar of the unchained winds. The arms of the warrior whom she loved are suspended over her head, and the mournful sound they produce as they clash, brings back to her heart the memory of her past happiness. Meanwhile, the lightening rives the clouds, and their livid light is reflected in her fixed eyes. Whilst the stake, whereon she is to be consumed, rises from the ground, alone, without consolation, in the stupor of despair, she awaits a frightful death, which a cruel prejudice causes her to prefer to life.

What a sweet and melancholy pleasure would any tender-hearted man experience in consoling this unfortunate! Whilst seated on the grass at her side,

I seek to dissuads her from the horrible sacrifice, and mingling my sighs with hers, and my tears with her tears, I endeavour to turn her thoughts from her grief, the whole town is hastening to the house of Mrs A——, whose husband has just died from a fit of apoplexy. Resolved not to survive her misfortune, insensible to the tears and prayers of her friends, she has determined to die of hunger ; and since early this morning, when the sad news was incautiously broken to her, the unfortunate woman has only eaten one biscuit and drunk one glass of Madeira. I only offer this despairing woman the mere attention requisite not to break through the rules of my universal system, and I leave her, as I am naturally jealous, and do not wish to be compromised with a crowd of consolers, or with persons too easy to console.

Unfortunate beauty has special claims on my heart, and the tribute of sensibility I owe them does not diminish the interest I bear to beauty joyful. This gives infinite variety to my pleasures, and enables me to pass from joy to melancholy, and from sentimental repose to enthusiasm.

Often also I form love intrigues in Ancient History, and cancel entire lines in the old registers of fate. How many times have I not stopped the paricidal hand of Virginius and saved the life of his unfortunate daughter, the victim at once of excess in crime and of excess in virtue ! This event fills me with terror when it recurs to my mind; I am not surprised that it was the origin of a revolution.

I hope that reasonable persons and compassionate souls will thank me for having settled this matter in a friendly way; and every man who has any knowledge of the world will agree with me that, had the Decemvir had his own way, this passionate man could not have failed to do justice to the virtue of Virginia; relations would have interfered; Father Virginius at last would have quieted down, and the marriage would have taken place according to all the forms required by law.

But what would have become of the unfortunate and neglected lover? Well, what did the lover gain by the murder? But, since you deign to have an interest in him, I will tell you, my dear Mary, that six months after the death of Virginia he was not only consoled but very happily married, and after having had several children, he lost his wife and married again, six weeks later, the widow of a tribune of the people. These circumstances, unknown till now, were discovered and deciphered in a Palimpsest MS in the Ambrosian library by a learned Italian antiquary. They will, unfortunately, increase by a page the abominable and already too protracted history of the Roman Republic.

XXIV. AFTER having saved the interesting Virginia, I modestly avoid her gratitude; and being always desirous of rendering some service to lovely woman, I profit by the obscurity of a rainy night and secretly open the tomb of a young vestal virgin, whom the Roman Senate has barbarously buried alive for having allowed the sacred fire of Vesta to go out—or, perhaps, for having got slightly burnt by it. Silently I tread the bye lanes of Rome, enjoying the inward delight which precedes good actions, especially when they are not without danger. I carefully avoid the Capitol for fear of awakening the geese, and, gliding through the Collina Gate, I happily reach the tomb without being perceived.

At the noise I make in raising the stone which covers her, the wretched woman lifts her dishevelled head from the damp floor of the vault. I see her by the light of the sepulchral lamp, casting around her looks distraught with terror: In her delirium, the unfortunate victim imagines herself already on the banks of the Cocytus:[1] "Oh Minos!" she cries, "oh inexorable judge! I loved, it is true, on earth, contrary to the severe laws of Vesta. If the gods are as barbarous as men, open, open for me the abyss of Tartarus! I loved and I love still." ——"No, no, thou art not yet in the kingdom of the dead; come, young and unfortunate woman, reappear on earth! revisit light and love." Meanwhile I seized her hand already frozen with the chill of the

---

[1] Cocytus, named of lamentation loud
Heard on the rueful stream.
---(MILTON'S PARADISE LOST. II.)

tomb; I took her in my arms, and, pressing her to my heart, I tore her away from this horrible spot, filled with terror and with gratitude.

Do not think, madame, that any personal interest actuated me in this good action. The hope of obtaining the favour of the lovely ex-vestal virgin entered in no wise into my calculations: I can assure you, on the word of a traveller, that during the whole of the walk from the Collina gate to the spot now occupied by the tomb of the Scipios, notwithstanding the darkness, and the fact that her weakness obliged her to lean on my arm, I never ceased to treat her with the respect and consideration due to her misfortunes, and I scrupulously returned her to her lover who was waiting for her on the road.

XXV. ANOTHER time, carried away by my reveries, I happened by chance to be present at the Rape of the Sabines: I saw, with much surprise, that the Sabines took the matter in quite a different spirit from that mentioned in history. Understanding nothing of the row that was going on, I offered my protection to a woman who was running away; and I could not help laughing, as I accompanied her, when I heard a furious Sabine warrior exclaim, with the accent of despair: "Ye immortal gods! why did I not bring my wife to the feast!"

XXVI. BESIDES that half of the human race to whom I bear so great an affection—shall I confess it, and will you believe me if I do?—my heart is endowed with such a capacity for tenderness, that every living thing, and even inanimate objects, have their share in it. I love the trees that give me shade, and the birds that sing in their branches, and the midnight shriek of the owl, and the sound of the torrents: I love everything . . . . . I love the moon!

You smile, miss: it is easy to turn into ridicule feelings one does not share: but hearts like mine will understand me.

Yes, I get attached to everything that surrounds me. I love the paths I tread, the spring I drink of; I cannot part without regret from the stick I have taken from the hedge as I passed; I look back after it when I have thrown it away; we had made friends; I regret the falling leaves, and even the passing zephyr. Where is now that zephyr which kissed thy black tresses, Eliza, when, seated by my side on the banks of the Doire, on the eve of our eternal separation, thou didst gaze on me in sorrowful silence? Where is thy look? Where is that painful, yet cherished, moment?

Oh time! terrible divinity! it is not thy cruel scythe which terrifies me; I fear only thy hideous children, indifference and forgetfulness, which turn into a long death three quarters of our existence.

Alas: that zephyr, that look, that smile, are as far away from one as the adventures of Ariadne: in the depths of my heart there remain only regrets and vain memories; a sad combination on which my life still floats, like a vessel, shattered by the tempest, still floats on the agitated sea! . . . . . .

XXVII. UNTIL, the water gradually penetrating through the leaking planks, the unfortunate ship disappears, engulfed in the abyss; the waves close over it, the tempest is calmed, and the sea-gull skims the solitary and tranquil plain of the ocean.

XXVIII. I FIND I must here close the explanation of my new method of love-making, as I perceive that it is verging on the dismal. It may not, however, be out of place to add a few more details on this discovery, which does not equally suit everybody and all ages. I would not advise any one to make use of it at twenty years of age. The inventor himself did not follow the system at that period. To make the most of it, one must have felt all the sorrows of life without being discouraged, and all its enjoyments without being surfeited. It is easy to follow my system, but it is especially useful at that age when reason advises us to give up the habits of our youth, and it can be made to act as a stepping-stone or bridge from pleasure to wisdom.

This crossing, as all moralists have observed, is extremely difficult. Few men have the noble courage to cross courageously; and often, after having passed over, they weary on the further bank, and recross the river, with grey hair and to their great shame. This they will easily be able to avoid by following my new system of love-making. In fact, most of our pleasures being only the results of imagination, it becomes necessary to offer this imagination some innocent prey to draw its attention off from objects which it should renounce, in the same way as parents offer toys to children when refusing them sweets. In this way one has time to take one's stand on the land of wisdom without noticing that one has yet reached it, and one travels there by the high road of folly, which will make it peculiarly easy to many people.

I do not think, then, that I have been mistaken in the hope of being useful, which hope induced me to take up my pen; and the only thing I have to guard against is a natural feeling of pride at having revealed to men truths of this nature.

XXIX. ALL these revelations, my dear Sophia, will not have caused you to forget, I hope, the awkward position in which you left me at my window. The emotion which the pretty foot of my neighbour had caused me still existed, and I had fallen more than ever under the dangerous influence of the slipper, when an unexpected event saved me from the peril in which I stood of throwing myself from the fifth storey into the street. A bat which was flying round the house, seeing me so long motionless, took me evidently for a chimney, and suddenly darted on me and seized me by the ear. I felt on my cheek the horrible cold of its damp wings. All Turin re-echoed with the involuntary shriek I uttered. The distant sentinels gave the alarm, and I heard in the street the hurried march of a patrol.

I left the view of the balcony without much regret; it no longer had any attraction for me. The chill of evening seemed to have seized me. I slightly shuddered; and as I drew my dressing gown round me, I sadly noticed that the cold and the bat's attack had been sufficient to again change the direction of my thoughts. The magic slipper would have had no more influence on me than Berenice's locks, or any other constellation. I at once saw how foolish it was to spend the night exposed to the cold, instead of following the law of nature which commands sleep. My reason, which then had alone any power over me, made this as clear as a proposition in Euclid. I was, in fact, suddenly deprived of imagination and enthusiasm, and given over bodily to sad reality. Wretched existence! One might as well be a dead tree in a forest, or an obelisk in a public square.

What strange machines, I cried, are the head and the heart of man! Carried away alternately in opposite directions by these two motive powers, the one he follows last always seems to him the best! Oh folly of enthusiasm and sentiment! says cold reason; oh weakness and uncertainty of reason! says sentiment. Who shall decide between them?

I thought it would be a good opportunity to decide which of these two guides it would be well to follow for the remainder of my life. Should it be my head or my heart? Let us examine the question.

XXX. SAYING these words, I noticed a dull pain in the foot which rested on the ladder step. I was, besides, very tired of the difficult position I had maintained up till then. I sat down gently; and, letting my legs hang to the right and left of the window, I continued my journey on horseback. I have always preferred this way of travelling to any other, and am passionately fond of horses. Nevertheless, out of all those I have ever seen or heard mentioned, the one I should prefer is the wooden horse spoken of in the Thousand and One Nights,[1] on

[1] Arabian Nights' Entertainment.

which one could travel through the air, and which sped away like lightning when you turned a little catch between its ears.

Now, you may notice that my steed greatly resembles that of the Thousand and One Nights. Owing to his position, he who travels on horseback on his window-sill communicates on one side with the heavens, and enjoys the imposing spectacle of nature; meteors and stars are at his disposal: on the other side, the sight of his dwelling and the objects it contains brings him back to the world. A turn of the head replaces the enchanted catch, and suffices to make in the traveller's soul a change as rapid as it is extraordinary. Inhabiting earth and heaven by turns, his mind and heart experience every enjoyment that is given to man.

I at once saw the advantage I could derive from my steed. When I felt myself comfortably in the saddle, certain of having nothing to fear from highwaymen or false steps on the part of my horse, I thought the opportunity a very favourable one to examine the problem I wished to solve touching the pre-eminence of reason or sentiment. But my first thought brought me to a standstill.

Is it for me to make myself judge in such a cause? For in my conscience I am already for a verdict in favour of sentiment. But again, if I exclude persons whose heart outweighs their head, whom shall I consult ? A geometrician? Bah ! Those fellows are sold body and soul to reason. To decide the point, a man should have received from nature an equal quantity of reason and sentiment, and, at the moment of deciding, these two faculties should be in perfect equilibrium . . . . An impossibility ! It would be easier to keep a republic in equilibrium.

The only competent judge, then, would be a man who would have nothing in common with either : a man without a head and without a heart. This extraordinary result was revolting to my reason ; my heart protested it had nothing to do with it. Yet it seemed to me I had reasoned logically, and I should at once have formed the worst idea of my intellectual faculties had I not reflected that, in high metaphysical speculations such as these, the greatest philosophers have often been led to frightful results which have had a great influence on human society.

I console myself, then, with the idea that my speculations will do harm to no one. I left the question undecided, and resolved, for the remainder of my days, alternately to follow my head and my heart. I fancy this is the best plan. It has not brought me a fortune as yet. Never mind, I still advance, descending the steep path of life without fear and without plans, laughing or weeping in turn, and sometimes both together, or whistling some old tune to pass the time away. Sometimes, I gather a daisy at the corner of a hedge ; I pull out the petals one after another, saying :

"She loves me little, much, passionately, not at all."[1] The last petal almost invariably brings *not at all.* In very truth, Eliza loves me no more.

Whilst I am thus occupied, the entire generation of the living passes away: like an immense wave it will soon dash with me on to the shore of eternity; and, as if the tempest of life was not fierce enough, as if it were urging us too gently towards the final barriers of existence, nations murder each other and forestall the date fixed by nature. Conquerors, themselves carried away by the rapid whirlwind of time, amuse themselves by slaughtering myriads of men. Hie! gentlemen, what are you thinking about? Wait a moment! All these good people were on the point of dying naturally. Do you not see the wave advancing? It already foams near the shore . . . . . Wait, in the name of Heaven, one moment only, and you, and your enemies, and I, and the daisies, we shall all have come to an end. Can one understand such madness! Come! one thing is settled; henceforth I myself will cease to destroy daises.

XXXI. AFTER having settled by means of my luminous logic, rules for my conduct in future, I had still one point to determine with regard to the journey I was undertaking. It is

[1] This is a favourite amusement with children and young people abroad, and resembles our own "Sortes Virgilianæ," of counting the cherry-stones, after eating cherry-pie, repeating, "I shall be married this year, next year, now or never."

not everything to get into a carriage or on horseback; one must also know where one is going to. I was so fatigued with my metaphysical researches that before deciding on the region of the globe to which I should give the preference I thought it best to rest and think of nothing at all. This is a way of living which I have also invented, and which has been of great use to me; but everyone cannot make use of it; for if it is easy to give depth to one's ideas by fixing one's thoughts perseveringly on a subject, it is not so easy to stop ones ideas suddenly like the pendulum of a clock. Molière has very foolishly ridiculed a man who amused himself in making circles with stones in the water of a well; I on the contrary should be inclined to think that man was a philosopher who had the power to suspend the action of his intelligence in order to rest, one of the most difficult operations the human mind can perform.

As this mode of existence powerfully favours the invasion of sleep, after half a minute's enjoyment I felt my head fall on my breast: I at once opened my eyes, and my ideas started afresh; a circumstance which evidently proves that this kind of voluntary lethargy is very different from sleep, as it was sleep that woke me; an accident which certainly never happened to any one else.

Raising my eyes, I perceived the polar star just above the house; this seemed to me a good omen on starting on a long journey. During the interval of rest I had enjoyed, my imagination had regained all its strength, and my heart was ready to receive the softest impressions; so much does a temporary annihilation of thought increase its energy! The feeling of sadness which my precarious worldly situation caused me was suddenly transformed into a powerful feeling of hope and courage; I found myself capable of daring life, and all the chances of misfortune and happiness it brings with it.

Brilliant star! I exclaimed in the delicious ecstasy which filled me, incomprehensible production of the Eternal Mind! Thou who alone, motionless in the sky, hast watched since the day of creation over half the earth! who directest the navigator over the deserts of the ocean, and a single sight of whom has often given back hope and life to the sailor pressed by the tempest! since I have never, when a clear night has allowed me to see the heavens, failed to seek thee amongst thy companions, assist me, celestial light! Alas! earth abandons me: be to-day my counsellor and my guide, and tell me what region of the globe I should fly to! During this invocation, the stars seemed to shine more brilliantly, and to rejoice in heaven, inviting me to trust to its protecting influence. I do not believe in presentiments; but I believe in a divine providence that leads men by unknown ways.

Each instant of our existence is a new creation, an act of the All-powerfull Will. I may even assert that I have sometimes perceived the imperceptible threads by means of which Providence makes the greatest men act like marionnettes, whilst they imagine they are leading the world ; a movement of pride it breathes into their hearts is sufficient to destroy armies, and to turn a nation upside down. However that may be, I believed so firmly in the reality of the invitation I had received from the polar star, that I immediately resolved to go north ; and although I had in these far-off regions neither preference nor real object, when I left Turin the next day, I went out by the Palace gate, to the north of the town, convinced that the polar star would not abandon me.

XXXII. I HAD reached this point of my journey, when I was obliged to get down hurriedly from my horse. I would not have mentioned this detail, were I not in conscience bound to inform the persons who may wish to adopt this mode of travelling of its little inconveniences, after having pointed out its immense advantages.

Windows, in general, not having been primitively invented for the new purpose I have put them to, architects in building them neglect to give them the commodious and rounded form of a saddle. The intelligent reader will understand, I hope, without further explanation, the painful cause which compelled me to make a halt. I got down with some difficulty, and took a turn or two up and down my room to stretch myself, reflecting on the mixture of pain and pleasure with which life is variegated, and on the kind of fatality which makes men the slaves of the most insignificant circumstances. After which I hastened to remount my horse, furnished with a sofa cushion, which I should not have dared do a few days before, for fear of being hooted by the cavalry; but having met the preceding day, at the gates of Turin, a party of Cossacks arriving on similar cushions from the banks of the Putrid and Caspian Seas, I thought I might, without violating the laws of horsemanship, which I greatly respect, adopt the same custom.

Delivered from the disagreeable sensation that I have hinted at, I was unable to give my mind to the details of my journey.

One of the difficulties that worried me most, because it was a matter of conscience, was to know if I was acting rightly or not in giving up my country, half of which had given me up.[1] Such a step seemed to me too important to be settled off-hand. Reflecting on the word native

[1] The author was serving in Piedmont, when Savoy, where he was born, was united to France.

land, I perceived I had no very clear idea of its meaning.

"My native land? What is my native land? Is it an assemblage of houses, of fields, of rivers? I cannot think so. Is it my family? Do my friends constitute my native land? But they have left it. Ah, I have it! It is the government. But it is changed. Good God! where, then, is my native land?" I passed my hand over my forehead in a state of inexpressible anxiety. The love of my native land is so fervent! The regrets I felt at the mere thought of leaving mine proved its existence so thoroughly that I would have remained on horseback all my life without dismounting rather than not have solved this difficulty.

I soon saw that the love of one's country depends on several circumsances—that is to say, on the long habit man gets into from his youth of being connected with the same individuals, the same locality, the same government. There only remained to examine how far these three causes contribute, separately, in making up one's native land.

The link which binds us to our fellow countrymen in general depends on the government, and is only the feeling of strength and happiness it gives us in common; for real affection is limited to the family and a small number of individuals immediately around us. Everything which breaks the habit or throws difficulty in the way of meeting men makes them enemies: A chain of mountains creates two peoples that dislike one another; the inhabitants of the right bank of a river think themselves far superior to those of the left bank, and the latter ridicule their neighbours in their turn. This disposition is noticed even in large towns cut by a river, notwithstanding the bridges which span it. The difference of language divides men still more. Lastly, the family itself, in which is centred our real affection, is often dispersed throughout our country; it continually changes its forms and numbers; besides which, it may be removed. It is, therefore, neither amongst our countrymen nor in our family that the love of our country is confined.

Locality contributes at least as much to the love we bear our native land. A very interesting question arises on this point: it has always been noticed that mountaineers, of all people, are most attached to their country, and that nomadic nations generally inhabit large plains. What can be the cause of this difference in the affection these people have for locality? If I mistake not, it is because amongst mountains one's native land has a physiognomy of its own, while it is not so in plains. It is a woman without features, and one cannot love her, in spite of all her good qualities. What, in fact, remains of his country for a villager to love when, inhabiting a wood-built hamlet, an enemy passes through, burning the village and cutting the trees? The wretch seeks in vain, along the uniform line of the horizon some known object wherewith to recall memories of the past: none exist. Each point of space offers him the same aspect and the same interest. This man is nomadic by nature unless the custom of his government holds him back; but his home will be here, there, anywhere; his native land is wherever the government exerts its power: he has only half a native land. The mountaineer loves tbe objects which meet his eyes from infancy, visible and indestructable forms: from every part of the valley, he can see and recognise his field on the side of the hill. The sound of the torrent, bubbling between the rocks, is never interrupted; the path that leads to the village swerves round an immovable block of granite. He sees in his dreams the outlines of the mountains, which are imprinted on his heart, just as, after having long looked at the panes of a window, one still sees them on closing one's eyes: The picture graven on his memory is part of himself, and cannot be effaced. Besides, memories themselves are connected with locality, but it must contain objects, the origin of which is unknown, or whose end cannot be foreseen. Old buildings, ancient bridges, everything which bears the character of greatness and long duration, takes the place, in part, of mountains: yet the monuments of nature have more power over the heart. To give to Rome a surname worthy of herself, the proud Romans called it the *City of the Seven Hills*. A habit, once formed, can never be destroyed. A middle-aged mountaineer can have no affection for the localities of a great city, and the inhabitant of cities cannot become a mountaineer. Hence it is, perhaps, that one of our greatest writers, who has painted with genius the deserts of America, found the Alps paltry, and Mont Blanc considerably too small.[1]

The share of government is evident. It is the first basis of one's native land. It is government which produces the reciprocal affection of men, and which renders more energetic the love they naturally bear to locality; government alone can, by memories of happiness or of glory, attach them to the soil whence they sprang.

If the government is good, the love of one's native land is in full vigour; if bad, love sickens; if it changes, it dies. It is then a new land, and each man can adopt it or choose another.

When the whole population of Athens quitted that city on the faith of Themistocles did the Athenians abandon their country, or did they carry it with them on to their ships?

When Coriolanus . . . .

Good God! into what discussion have I drifted! I forget that I am on horseback on my window-sill.

XXXIII. I HAD an old relation of much wit, whose conversation was extremeiy interesting; but her memory, inconstant though

[1] Gustave Aymard.

fertile, often made her pass from episode to episode, and from digression to digression, till she was forced to implore the help of her auditors: "What was I going to tell you?" she used to say; and often her auditors had forgotten it also, which threw the whole company into inexpressible embarrassment. Now, you may have remarked that the same accident often happens to me in my narrative, and I confess that the plan and order of my journey are traced on the identical plan of my aunt's conversation; but I ask assistance of no one, because I perceive that my subject comes back of its own accord at the very moment I expect it least.

XXXIV. THOSE persons who do not approve of my treatise on the subject of native lands, must be warned that for some time past sleep has been creeping over me, notwithstanding my efforts to keep awake. Nevertheless, I am not quite sure now whether I fell fast asleep, and whether the extraordinary events I am about to relate were the effect of a dream or of a supernatural vision.

I saw a brilliant cloud descend from heaven and approach me by degrees, covering, as with a transparent veil, a young woman twenty-two or twenty-three years of age. I know not how to describe the feelings which her aspect gave birth to. Her face, sparkling with goodness and kindness, had all the charms of youth's illusions, and was soft as the dreams of the future. Her look, her peaceful smile, all her features, in a word, realised in my eyes the ideal being sought for so long by my heart, and whom I had despaired of meeting.

While I watched her in delightful ecstasy, I saw the polar star through her black tresses, fluttering in the wind, and at the same moment I heard these consoling words. Words, do I say? It was the mysterious expression of the Divine Mind unveiling the future to my intelligence; it was a prophetic communication from the protecting star I had invoked, and the sense of which I will try to render in human words.

"Thy confidence in me shall not be betrayed," said a voice whose tone resembled the sound of Æolian harps. "Behold this is the land I have reserved for thee; this is the gem men aspire to, who think that happiness is a calculation, and ask of the earth what can only be obtained from Heaven." At these words, the meteor returned into the depths of space, and the celestial divinity was lost in the mists of the horizon; but, as she retired, she cast on me glances which filled my heart with confidence and hope.

Immediately, burning to follow her, I put spurs to my horse with all my might; but, as I had forgotten to put on spurs, I struck my right heel against the angle of a tile so violently, that pain woke me up with a start.

XXXV. THIS accident was a real advantage for the geological portion of my journey, as it gave me the opportunity of ascertaining exactly the height of my room above the layer of alluvial soil on which the town of Turin is built.

My heart beat fast, and I had just counted three and a half beats, from the time I had spurred my horse, when I heard the fall of my slipper into the street, which, having closely calculated the time which heavy bodies take in falling, and that occupied by the transmission of sonorous undulations through the air from the street to my ear, gives a height from the level of the Turin pavement to my window of 94 feet, 3 lines, and 19-20ths of a line, supposing my heart, agitated by the dream, was beating 120 to the minute, which cannot be far from the truth. It is only for the sake of science that, after speaking of the interesting slipper of my beautiful neighbour, I venture to mention mine: I therefore warn you that this chapter is strictly intended for the learned.

XXXVI. THE brilliant vision I had experienced made me feel all the more, on awakening, the horror of the isolation in which I found myself. I cast my eyes around and saw nothing but roofs and chimneys. Alas! suspended up at the fifth story between heaven and earth, surrounded with an ocean of regrets, desires, and anxieties, an uncertain gleam of hope alone bound me to existence; a fantastic support the fragility of which I have but too often experienced. Doubt re-entered my heart, still bleeding with the disappointments of life, and I firmly believed that the polar star had been laughing at me. Unjust and guilty suspicion, for which the heavenly body punished me by ten years of waiting! Oh, if I had only foreseen then that all these promises would be accomplished, and that I should one day meet again on earth the adored being whose image I had only caught a glimpse of in the sky! Dear Sophia, if I had known that my happiness would surpass all my hopes! but I must not anticipate events. I return to my subject, not wishing to interrupt the methodical and severe regularity of the plan I have followed in the narrative of my journey.

XXXVII. THE clock in the tower of the Church of St Philip slowly tolled midnight. I counted each stroke, and the last drew a sigh from me. "There is another day," said I, "gone from my life;" and although the decreasing vibrations of the brazen bell still resound in my ear, that part of my voyage preceding midnight is as far from me as the voyages of Ulysses or Jason. In this abyss of the past, seconds and centuries are equal; and has the future more reality? I am standing poised between two precipices, as it were on the edge of a sword. Time, indeed, seems to me something so inconceivable, that I am tempted to think it does not really exist, and that what is so named is only a punishment of the mind.

I was rejoicing at having found this definition for time, as incomprehensible as time itself, when another clock struck midnight, which caused me a disagreeable sensation. I am always somewhat irritable when I have been working at an insoluble problem, and I thought this second warning from a clock, to a philosopher like myself, extremely out of place. But I was simply disgusted, a few seconds later, when I heard in the distance a third clock, that of the Convent of the Capucines, on the other bank of the Po, strike midnight, as if out of spite.

When my aunt used to call her old and somewhat cross lady's maid, whom she was very fond of, she was not satisfied, in her impatience, with ringing once, but she pulled the bell-rope incessantly till her maid appeared. "Come on, Mademoiselle Branchet!" and the latter, angry at being hurried, came leisurely, and answered sharply, before entering the drawing room: "Coming, Ma'am, coming." Such was the feeling of irritation I felt, when I heard the indiscreet clock of the Capucines ringing out midnight for the third time. "I know it, I know it," cried I, stretching my hands towards the clock; "I know that it is midnight: I know it but too well."

. . . .

It is, undoubtedly, on the advice of the Evil Spirit, that men have fixed on that hour to divide their days. Shut up in their homes, they sleep or enjoy themselves, whilst it cuts one of the threads of their existence: the next day they rise joyfully, not dreaming the least in the world, that they are a day older. In vain does the prophetic sound of the clock warn them of the approach of Eternity; in vain does it sadly remind them of each hour as it passes; they hear nothing, or if they hear, they understand not. Oh midnight! terrible hour! I am not superstitious, but this hour ever inspired me with a kind of fear, and I feel that, if I ever die, it will be at midnight. Then I shall die some day? What! *I* die! *I*, who speak, who feel; can *I* die? I have some difficulty in believing it: for, after all, that others should die is perfectly natural: one sees that every day: we see them pass by, and get accustomed to it; but to die one's self! to die bodily! that is rather too much. And you, gentlemen, who look upon these reflections as rubbish, learn that every one thinks this, you amongst the number. No man thinks that he has to die. If there existed a race of immortals, this idea of death would frighten them more than it does us.

There is something in this which I do not understand. How is it that men, ever agitated with hope, or with the mirages of Future, take so little thought of the only certain and inevitable event the Future has in store for them? May it not be that beneficent Nature itself has given us this happy indifference, so that we may in peace fulfil our destiny? I believe, indeed, that one can be a very good fellow without adding, to the real evils of life, that turn of thought which leads to gloomy reflections, and without troubling one's imagination with black phantoms. Lastly, I think one should laugh, or smile at any rate, whenever an innocent opportunity offers.

. . . .

Thus ends the meditation inspired by the clock of St. Philip's. I should have pushed it further if some scruples had not arisen in my mind as to the morality of my conclusions. But, unwilling to examine this doubt, I whistled the *Follies of Spain*,[1] which has the power of changing my thoughts when they go astray. The effect was so prompt, that I at once brought my ride to an end.

---

[1] A favorite air at the end of the eighteenth century.

XXXVIII. BEFORE re-entering my room, I cast a glance over the town and darkened neighbourhood of Turin, that I was about to leave, perhaps for ever, and bid them a last farewell. Never had night appeared so lovely; never had the view before me so interested me. After having saluted the mountain and temple of Superga, I took leave of the towers, steeples, and all known objects I never thought I could regret so much, of the air, the sky, and the river whose soft ripple seemed to re-echo my adieux. Oh! if I could paint the feelings, tender and cruel, which filled my heart, and all the memories of the best half of my life, which crowded round me, like so many will-o'-the-wisps, to retain me at Turin! but, alas! memories of past happiness are the wrinkles of the soul! when we are unhappy, we must drive them from our thoughts as mocking phantoms deriding our present situation: it is a thousand times better than to give one's self up to the deceitful illusions of hope; especially is it necessary to put a good face on the matter, and to admit no one into the secret of one's misfortunes. I have noticed, in my ordinary journeys amongst men, that by dint of being unfortunate one becomes ridiculous. In those dreadful moments, nothing can be more suitable than the new method of travelling I have described. I found it so, undoubtedly. Not only did I succeed in forgetting he past, but I was even able to look my present troubles in the face. Time will carry them away, I thought; he carries everything away; he forgets nothing; and whether we try to hurry or to restrain him, our efforts are alike vain, and cannot change his changeless course. Although I seldom notice his rapid flight, some circumstance, some train of thought, recalls it to me in a striking manner. It is when men are silent, when the demon of noise is dumb in the midst of his temple, in the midst of a slumbering city, it is then that Time raises his voice, and is heard by my soul. Silence and darkness become his interpreters, and unveil to me his mysterious flight; he is no longer a being my mind cannot comprehend: he becomes visible to my thoughts; I see him in the skies, driving the stars towards the west. Behold him chasing the rivers to the sea, and rolling over the hills with the mists! . . . . Listen! the winds howl under the pressure of his rapid wings, and the distant bell tolls his passing knell!

"Let us profit, let us profit by his course," I cried. "I will make good use of the seconds he will rob me of." Wishing to carry out this good resolution, I at once leant forward to urge on my steed, making with my tongue a certain noise which was never meant to hurry horses forward, but which cannot be written according to any rules of orthography: "Gh! gh! gh!" and I finished my ride with a gallop.

XXXIX. I WAS raising my right foot to get off my horse, when I felt a somewhat sharp blow on my shoulder. To say I was not frightened at this event would be untrue; and here occurs an opportunity of pointing out to the reader, and of proving to him, how difficult it would be for anyone but myself to execute a similar journey. Supposing another traveller had a thousand times more means and talents for observation than I had, could he flatter himself with the prospect of such peculiar, such numerous adventures, as those which have happened to me within four hours, and which are undoubtedly the result of my destiny? If anyone doubts this, let him try to guess who struck me. In the first moment of emotion, forgetting the position I was in, I thought my horse had reared, or had struck me against a tree. Heaven knows how many terrible thoughts passed through my mind during the second it took me to turn my head to look into my room. I then saw, as usually happens in what appears most extraordinary, that the cause of my surprise was a very natural one: The same puff of wind which, at the beginning of my journey, had opened my window and closed my door as it passed, and part of which had slipped in between the curtains of my bed, had noisily re-entered my room. It roughly opened the door and went out of the window, pushing the frame against my shoulder, which caused the surprise I have mentioned.

You will recollect that it was on the invitation of this puff of wind that I had left my bed. The shock I had just experienced was evidently an invitation to return to it, which I thought myself compelled to accept.

It is a fine thing, no doubt, to be thus in familiar intercourse with the night, the sky and the meteors, and to know how to profit by their influence. Ah! the intercourse one is compelled to have with men is far more dangerous! How many times have I not been the dupe of my confidence in these gentlemen! I had even mentioned something of this subject in a note which I have suppressed, because it happened to to be rather longer than the text itself, which would have damaged the proper proportions of my journey, the shortness of which is its greatest merit.

THE END.

Printed by E. & G. Goldsmid, Edinburgh.

MIDNIGHT HORRORS;

OR,

THE BANDIT'S DAUGHTER.

AN ORIGINAL ROMANCE.

NEW-YORK.

PUBLISHED BY W. BORRADAILE,

And sold Wholesale and Retail, at his Book-store,

130 FULTON-STREET.

1823.

MIDNIGHT HORRORS;

OR,

THE BANDIT'S DAUGHTER.

THE deep-toned clock of a dilapidated and deserted priory, striking the fear-fraught hour of midnight, sounded with prophetic horror on the ear of the Baroness di Montalban, whilst a foreboding dread of some impending, some unknown ill, sat heavy at her heart. Twice had the sun performed its yearly course, since the lady of Montalban had beheld the beloved of her bosom.

Called by honour to the scene of warfare, the heart of the baron now swelled with military ardour, now sank with tender regret, as he strained, in a farewell embrace, the faithful partner of his cares and joys; nor less did the gentle Gertrude deplore the separation.

No sound of merriment vibrated through the gothic castle of Montalban; scarcely a smile brightened on the features of the baroness, during the tedious absence of her lord.

The campaign had concluded; but the Baron di Montalban had bled in the cause of his country; and the danger attending his wound permitted him not to return to the seat of his ancestors. The lady Gertrude, distracted with apprehension, allowed no selfish consideration to delay the progress of her journey towards the unsolaced couch of her wounded lord; and though the night's drear shade had long enveloped the blooming face of nature, as they gained the gloomy precincts of the forest, the baroness still determined to proceed. Reluctant to disappoint the impatience, and dispute the command, of the mistress whom they loved and reverenced, the domestics slowly guided the carriage through the mazy intricacies, whilst the convulsive trembling of their frames, as their strained eye-balls sought to pierce the deepening gloom, spoke the apprehensive terror that agitated their hearts.

The rising blast sounded in hollow breathings through the

leafy branches of the waving trees. whilst night's pale orb, concealed by an immense cloud, refused to lighten with her silver beams the windings of the dubious way; the faint lights that quivered in the lamps of the carriage. and the torches borne in the unsteady hands of two of the domestics, dimmed by the rude wind that swept across the forest, were ill able to direct the travellers in their course.

The mind of the baroness, enervated by fear and anxiety for the fate of Montalban's chieftain, was ill able to support with firmness the gloomy horrors of the lonely scene, which she now repented having determined to encounter. Each object that started on her sight became an image of terror; phantoms of horrific forms appeared gliding through the interstices of the trees; whilst the mournful howling of the blast seemed to sound upon her starting ear, as the dying groans of the absent Di Montalban. But soon each ideal form of imagined horror yielded to a dread reality; the shrilly notes of the banditti's horn filled up the pauses of the wind; and soon the loud trampling of approaching steeds, reverberated along the various paths that led through the forest. Each heart, palsied with the conviction of immediate danger, now sank in the panting bosom of the travellers; whilst the chilled blood, recoiling from their eyes and cheeks, left every feature imprinted with the fearful characters of terror and dismay. Impelled by a faint hope of safety, they turned to retrace their steps; but soon their pursuers, with superior speed. baffled the expectation. The carriage was surrounded, and the insensible baroness rudely seized by the ruffian band. The sight rekindled in the breast of her domestics the courage which terror had damped but not annihilated; each drew a glittering sabre from its scabbard, and vigorously prepared to repel the attack of their muscular opponents; but, unequal to the contest, one after another, the brave vassals of the Lady di Montalban fell in her cause; and the remaining few. unable longer to contend against a foe so powerful, surrendered to the triumphant crew.

The baroness had revived for a few moments during the conflict, and, fearful of the event. she sprang from the carriage, fondly trusting to the possibility of eluding by flight the dreaded and unknown fate that might await her, as a captive to the daring gang; but, alas! fallacious was the hope; the broad glare of the numerous torches revealed her to the view of the banditti. and the ill fated wife of Montalban was seized by one of the desperadoes, and re-conducted to the carriage; but not till, in her efforts to free herself from the rude grasp of her ruthless conductor, she received an accidental wound from the unsheathed weapon he continued to carry in his hand.

Life's common tide ebbed swiftly through the gaping wound, and again each agonized thought became absorbed in insensibility. The inanimate baroness was replaced in the carriage; and one of the men, stationing himself by her side, another took the seat of the driver, and slowly conducted it towards that part of the forest in which their habitation was situated. An iron door, covered with earth, so as to appear like the ground of the forest, admitted the band to a long subterraneous cavity, terminating in a gloomy cavern, of large dimensions; two lamps, suspended from the centre of the ceiling, but imperfectly displayed the extremities of the immense chamber, and threw a hideous glare on the ferocious countenances and uncouth dresses of the banditti.

An old man, who was in the capacity of a servant, and whose every feature betrayed the hardened callousness of his nature, was desired by the chieftain of the band to fetch restoratives for the insensible Lady di Montalban, and to make the preparations which were necessary to dress the wound.

At length the ill fated captive unclosed her languid eyes, but the vacant stare with which she gazed around, the calm placidity with which she suffered the approaches of the forbidding objects by which she was surrounded, plainly evinced that reason lingered, though animation had returned. Careless of her fate, the chieftain but slightly attended to the dressing of her wound; and summoning Eglantine, the only female residing in the cavern, he directed her to attend the senseless baroness to the apartment allotted her.

The heavy stupor that pervaded the senses of the Lady di Montalban calming the agitation of her mind, her eyes soon closed in a long refreshing slumber; and when she again opened them, it was to a sad, though imperfect consciousness of the horrors of her situation; for a few moments she gazed wildly around, but soon her eyes ceased their wandering; attracted by a form of such seraphic beauty, a countenance of such heavenly sweetness, that their rivetted attention seemed ever fixed! Tall and slender was the figure that bent o'er her couch with tender and fearful solicitude! no form could be modelled with a symmetry more perfect; no features beamed with an expression of more angelic innocence; the softest blush of the rose blended with the lily on her cheek, and heightened the brilliancy of her dark-blue eyes, beaming with every attribute of heaven-born worth; of golden hue were the long and beautiful tresses that partially shaded her polished forehead, and flowed in careless clusters of luxuriant curls upon a bosom white as snow. A simple vesture of white, ornamented with pearls, encircled her slender form, over which a loose robe, fastened on the bosom by a silver clasp, and confined round the waist by a zone of the same metal, fell in negligent folds to her feet. "Fair vision of celestial brightness!" exclaimed the baroness, still gazing on the countenance of Eglantine, "wherefore hast thou deigned to visit this blood-stained mansion of sanguinary guilt? If aught to me imports thy heavenly vision, O! quick reveal the sacred purpose." "Lady, my comprehension takes not thy meaning," returned Eglantine; "I have ever dwelt within this cavern, and have no purpose in visiting thee, but pity for thy illness, and the hope of promoting, by my care, thy restoration. My name is Eglantine; I am the chieftain's daughter." "Wonderful!" exclaimed the Lady di Montalban, "that such heavenly prints should spring uncontaminated from a a source so noxious."

"I have prepared thy morning repast, lady," said Eglantine, inattentive to the apostrophe of the baroness, "which I trust thou wilt find refreshing." The baroness took the proferred food from the fair hand of the beauteous maid, for whom she had imbibed an interest so tender, that, for a moment, the acuteness of her own regret yielded to the deep concern she felt in the fate of the young and innocent stranger.

"And art thou, sweet Eglantine, the only female in this desolate retreat?" enquired the baroness. "Alas! yes, lady!" replied Eglantine. "Dame Jacquelina died a twelvemonth since; she was my nurse, lady; I shall never, never forget her! she was so fond, and so good to me; and then, when my father chided, and treated me unkindly, she would let me weep on her bosom, and speak consolation to me; but now (she added with a sigh) I have no. no kind nurse to love, and sooth me!" "And did not Dame Jacquelina offer to instruct thee; to awaken in thy mind a sense of thy dangerous situation?" asked the Lady Gertrude: "did she not point out to thee various circumstances relative to the beings with whom thou hast been fated to associate?" "O! no lady," said Eglantine, "my dear nurse never told me aught to make me fearful, or to give me pain; she taught me submission to my father's will. O! she was very good, and she strove to make me like herself. Whole hours have I listened, in this apartment, this very apartment, to her kind instructions. Sometimes she would talk to me, and tell me what was right, and what was wrong; and sometimes she would teach me to sing and play upon the lute; and I was so happy; but I shall never be so happy again." "Heaven forbid!" exclaimed the baroness with energy. "O Eglantine! I tremble for thy fate! so young, so beautiful, and so innocent; to herd with a race so pityless and uncongenial. Alas! I fear the guardian of thy inexperienced youth failed to impress upon thy unsuspicious mind the dread conviction of a parent's errors! Sweet child of innocent simplicity! on me shall the painful task devolve."

"What mean'st thou, lady?" Eglantine earnestly demanded; the rich suffusion fading from her cheek.—"Didst thy instructress e'er speak to thee of banditti, of lawless plunderers, and unprovoked assassins?" enquired the baroness. "No, lady; I know not what they mean."

The baroness sighed: she felt at that moment too faint, and too little prepared for a task so painful, so arduous, to venture on the instruction she premeditated giving, and Eglantine shortly after quitting the melancholy chamber, with her sweet form, seemed to vanish the new ideas that had cheated her awhile from the contemplation of her own sorrows.

Though the blood had issued so copiously from the side of the baroness, the wound was slight, and extreme faintness was now the only effect she experienced from the accident; and as fancy again conjured up the expiring form of her lord, she determined not to delay her resolution of imparting to the bandit's daughter, the intended communication; trusting to impress her mind with so just an abhorrence of the ruffian band, with whom she had hitherto resided, unsuspicious of guile, as to inspire her with a desire to aid her (the baroness's) escape from the cavern, and to participate in her flight.

The day wore dull and heavily away, it seemed to the Lady Montalban a long and dismal night; no cheering beam of day's bright luminary pierced the darksome chambers of the subterranean habitation; and the dim solitary lamp, that burnt on the dark oak table, cast a melancholy shade on each surrounding object.

Eglantine tended her through the day; but the baroness found it impossible to execute her purpose, from one of the men who, by the desire of the chieftain, accompanied his daughter to the chamber of the wounded captive.

The sweet maid, long unaccustomed to the presence of a being of her own sex, panted for the society of the baroness, uninterrupted by the presence of Rodolpho. The language of the Lady di Montalban had awakened in her mind a restless curiosity; and when the usual hour of retiring led the inmates of the cavern to their respective pallets, Eglantine, instead of seeking repose, with a light step quitted her chamber, and hastened to that of the baroness.

Most grateful to the Lady Gertrude was the presence of the lovely fair. Sleep had refused to shed its soothing influence o'er her senses; and her mind, agonized by past joys, and an anticipation of future ills, seemed incapable of supporting the horrors of a long night, passed in solitude and harassed reflections.

Varied and painful were the emotions that swelled the bosom of the guileless Eglantine, as the Lady di Montalban unfolded to the shuddering maid the sanguinary means by which the remorseless crew amassed the wealth secreted in the dreary cavern. The baroness, fearful of too severely wounding the susceptible feelings of the tender maid, by precipitately awakening her to a full sense of the horror of murder and rapine, forbore to delineate, with a too minute precision, the dreadful picture.

The heart of the youthful Eglantine had never throbbed with filial tenderness for the haughty chieftain of the band; her gentle spirit had revolted at his harsh commands, and timidly shrank from his stern countenance, and the heavy frown that sat upon his gloomy brow; and when, on the day she had numbered her eighteenth year, he ordered her to consider the second in command, the Signor Gonsalvo, as her future lord, she yielded a consent she dared not to withhold—yet trembled to fulfil.

With the nurse of her infancy, the friend, the companion of her riper years, seemed to have expired the warm affections of her soul. No object in the spacious cave now boasted an attraction to the chilled heart of Eglantine, excepting the cold receptacle in which withered the mouldering form of Jacquelina, till the ill-fated Lady di Montalban became a captive in the immolating cavern. Her distress, her tenderness, and sex awaked the dormant feelings that had slumbered in the affectionate bosom of the young recluse, and made the task of persuasion easy to the baroness.

Eglantine, ever shrinking with horror from the projected union of herself and Gonsalvo, to which the communication of the Lady di Montalban had added ten-fold repugnance; and more influenced by fear than affection, in her conduct towards her father, was easily induced by the entreaties of the baroness, to endeavour to accelerate, and join in her escape.

On the ensuing night, when sleep should have closed the eyes of the banditti, Eglantine promised to conduct the Lady di Montalban along the private passages leading thro' the subterranean dwelling; of which she, unknown to her sire, possessed some imperfect knowledge.

Eglantine had by accident discovered the unfrequented way, during the life-time of Dame Jacquelina; but that tender friend, ever fearful for the happiness of her charge, warned her not to reveal the knowledge she had unpremeditatedly obtained; secretly believing, that, at some future period, she might have reason to avail herself of the unknown discovery.

At the appointed hour, as soon as the band, worn out with the fatigues of the day, had sunk into the arms of sleep, and an undisturbed silence reigned around, Eglantine, with a light faltering step, repaired to the chamber of the baroness. Already was the Lady di Montalban ready to receive her; and scarcely daring to speak, fearful even of the faintest sound betraying them to the banditti, they passed towards the great hall.

Eglantine had enveloped her lovely form in a long wrapping cloak of sable hue, and presented a similar one to the baroness.

The strong emotions that shook the trembling frame of the Bandit's daughter, as, for the last time, she paced the only home she had ever known, retarded their progress through the numerous caverns and passages that led to the secret opening.

Though Eglantine had reflected with disgust and terror on the partially revealed characters of her associates, and though she had dwelt with delight on the ideal picture of future joy, pourtrayed in the promises of the Lady di Montalban; yet, when the hour of flight drew nigh, a hesitating reluctance arose in her gentle bosom. Every spot seemed endeared to her as the scene of her childhood, and as bringing to her mind some tender recollection of the beloved Jacquelina. Her father too!—at the moment of final separation, the stern chieftain, the haughty superior, seemed lost in the recollection of his paternal character.

The baroness beheld, in the quivering lip of her young companion, the faded cheek, and the frequent drop that rolled from the soft blue eye, the conflict of her mind; and too interested in the fate of the sweet maid, to view with satisfaction the prospect of her own escape unaccompanied, had again recourse to those arguments she had so before successfully exerted. The effort was not successless; Eglantine arose from the seat in which she had involuntarily sunk, and with a quicker step, moved forward.

The passages they were then traversing terminated in a large iron door, fastened by a rusty lock, in which the key was still remaining. The Lady di Montalban assisted the trembling hand of Eglantine to unclose it; it grated with a low, creaking sound, as it slowly opened, that vibrated dismally on the fearful hearts of the timid fugitives A short flight of black steps were on the inner side. Eglantine lowered her light, as they carefully descended. A violent gust of wind rushed through the cavern into which they were admitted, that nearly extinguished the quivering flame; and the baroness, imagining it to be occasioned by a current of air, reclosed the iron door. The light of the lamp again became steady; and Eglantine, raising it to take a minute survey of the cave they had entered, found, with inconceivable distress, that she retained not the faintest recollection of the gloomy spot on which she then stood. Conjecturing, that she had been deceived by the similarity of the last passage to the one she ought to have pursued, she imparted to the trembling baroness the discovery; who, anxious to quit a place in which every object bore an appearance of gloomy terror, and fearful of the danger of delay, they re-ascended to the door by which they had entered; but the lock had re-fastened, and the key being left on the other side, the possibility of returning was entirely precluded. The Lady di Montalban and the trembling Eglantine for a few moments gazed on each other with inexpressible anguish and dismay.

The baroness first recovered; and taking the lamp from the hand of her companion, she gazed wishfully around, in the hope of discovering some other door or aperture by which they might pursue their way —It was a small square cavern, whose dark, uncleanly walls, exhibited various pondrous weapons covered with rust and mildew. The only furniture, a large black table in the center, covered with a pall of sable velvet, on which the worms and other reptiles had been permitted to make unnumbered depredations. Several niches on either side exhibited to the recoiling view of the shuddering pair the fleshless forms of their fellow beings, fastened by chains round the middle, neck, and ancles, to the walls!—A pitcher of water and a mouldy loaf of bread were placed at a short distance from the reach of each. The baroness imagined, as she gazed on the dreadful receptacle, and read the motto imprinted in characters of blood over the head of each, that they had been condemned by the merciless judges of their fate, to perish; wanting the food that, even to the last moment, was permitted to remain within their sight!

"BEHOLD THE FATE OF A TRAITOR, AND TREMBLE!" was the fearful motto. Turning from a scene too repugnant to the tender feelings of humanity for a longer contemplation, the attention of the baroness and Eglantine became rivetted to a large black curtain that, descending from the roofing of the cavern, flowed in long sable folds to the flooring of a high raised platform, to which a half-decayed flight of stone steps, corresponding with those that led to the cave, were affixed in the center. The sable hue of the curtain, rendered more gloomy by the faint rays of the lamp that beamed on it a pale dismal hue, inspired a chilly sensation of terror, as fancy pictured the unknown something it might conceal, that thrilled painfully through the trembling frames of the Lady di Montalban and the pallid Eglantine. In vain they searched, with the minutest scrutiny, the other sides of the apartment; not the slightest aperture or appearance of a door greeted the eyes of the anxious examiners.

Again the wind whistled through the subterranean building, and the curtain was shaken by the rudeness of the blast;—the momentary terror the sight inspired, quickly yielded to the hope that behind its darksome folds was concealed some friendly outlet. The native firmness of the Lady di Montalban revived, as the solacing idea flashed on her harassed mind; and hastily ascending the steps, she trod with a steady foot upon the platform. Eglantine followed with a faltering pace the steps of the baroness, as with instinctive terror she crept closely to her side.

Already was the cord, by which the curtain was at will suspended, in the hand of the baroness: but scarcely had she drawn it a few inches through the rusty wheel, ere a groan, such as might issue from the lips of expiring nature, sounded on their startled ears, and died in a hollow murmur through the vaulted cavern. Incapable of proceeding further, the nerveless hand of the baroness dropped the cord it had grasped with such determined firmness; and the lamp at the same moment falling to the ground, the oil was so nearly expended, that the unfed flame served merely to increase the horror of the scene. Eglantine had sunk on her knees, and with her cold trembling arms encircled the form of the baroness; every feature was distorted with agony; her eyes wildly glared around the dreary chamber, now nearly involved in darkness; her lips and cheeks were bloodless; and her panting bosom heaved with convulsive emotions. An awful pause of unbroken silence succeeded to the fearful groan that had echoed through the dreary cavern; when another, even more dismal than the first, followed by a third, reverberated through the cave. The curtain as though guided by some invisible hand, was slowly raised from the platform towards the roofing, at the same moment, the lamp, emitting a faint beam, expired.

A pale blue vapour issuing from the extremity, gradually diffused a stronger light on the object that the veiling curtain had concealed, and revealed a narrow and deep chasm, in which were deposited, in rude disorder, a number of coffins. A ladder, placed in nearly a perpendicular direction, led into the interior of the dreary sepulchre.

The vapour had dispersed, and the light had collected itself into a small ball of steady flame, that gliding slowly through the air, stationed itself over the yawning cavern.—Several minutes elapsed ere the minds of the baroness and Eglantine could regain sufficient composure to allow of reflection. At length, the Bandit's daughter arose from her kneeling position, and the Lady Gertrude withdrawing herself from the pillar against which her enervated form had reclined, ventured, with a hesitating step, to draw nearer to the brink of the tomb. The sharp current of air that passed through the dreary receptacle, blew with reviving coolness;—the desire of escape again predominated over terror; and, confident that their only hope of liberation depended on their passing through the vault, the baroness, endeavouring to revive the fainting courage of her timid companion, prepared to descend into the dread abyss.

Eglantine, as she beheld the firmness of her guide, and reflected on the guileless tenor of her life, felt her bosom inspired with renovated fortitude; and breathing a short prayer to the Being on whose mercy she had ever relied for protection, she followed the footsteps of the baroness. A few moments conducted them to the last step of the ladder, and they found themselves in a narrow passage, formed by a row of coffins on either side, and at irregular distances obstructed by fragments of others, that time had decayed, and nearly crumbled into dust. Traces of blood were visible in several places; and not unfrequently the baroness and Eglantine found their progress impeded by human skulls and bones that had escaped the narrow confines of their mouldering prisons! The blue flame that had revealed the contents of the spacious chasm ere they entered, had descended with them, and had continued to guide them through the mansions of the dead.

The silent fugitives, with awful wonder, beheld the supernatural conductor, whilst the persuasion of its being the interference of a benignant Providence to direct them on their doubtful course, inspired a pious enthusiasm, that quelled their fears, and gave firmness to their steps. The vault ended in a low range of coffins, over which it was necessary to climb, in order to proceed. The baroness still led the way; and with a light step trod on the cold receptacles of "the unhonoured dead;" the decayed appearances of which rendering caution necessary, they paused a moment, as they gained the top, to discern the opposite side, and beheld with inconceivable delight, an iron grating that, half unclosed, admitted the violent draught of air which had been the primary cause of their traversing the darksome regions they were then exploring. Encouraged by the view, again they proceeded. When Eglantine, stepping on the coffin that stood next, the lid, which had appeared capable of supporting her weight, gave way; and she found one of her feet entangled in the skeleton legs of the body it contained. Stepping forward, in her efforts to disengage herself, the affrighted maid fell on the stiffened form; and felt, with recoiling horror, the fleshless cheek in contact with her own. With a violent effort, and almost distracted, Eglantine disentangled herself from the narrow prison of the mouldering bones; and, forgetful of the baroness, of every thing, but the recent terror she had encountered, flew towards the grating, and hastily swinging it on its hinges, ran breathless through several of the caverns to which it led. She was now proceeding in total darkness, but the horror of her mind rendered her unconscious of her situation; she hurried forward with unremitted speed, till her exhausted strength being no longer able to support her, she sank in a state of insensibility upon the ground. Several minutes elapsed, ere respiration again heaved the cold bosom of the senseless fair; and it was not till some seconds after her eyes unclosed, that a full consciousness of the past dawned upon her mind.

A recollection of the baroness now crossed her mind: and the fear of losing her became the predominant cause of terror; she determined, if possible, to group her way along the dark windings, through which she had so hastily fled; after searching for some time, she found there was one large opening in the cave; and cheered by the discovery, since she must necessarily pass through it, she proceeded down a long passage, twining in a serpentine direction. Eglantine had not proceeded far, ere her hand struck upon the iron grating, and she paused, to listen if aught of the baroness could be heard; but no sound met her ear; as she gazed around, she thought she beheld at a distance, a gleam of the mysterious light that she had parted from in quitting the sepulchre; and following with a quick step the direction in which it appeared to move, she soon found herself at a second grating, and on turning a sudden angle, to her inexpressible relief, she discovered the baroness.

Eglantine, in a moment threw herself on the bosom of the Lady di Montalban; and was fondly encircled in a fervent embrace; then raising her eyes, she beheld, with emotions of delight and gratitude, the secret door that led to the forest, on which the friendly light shone with refulgent brightness.—Quickly she drew the fastenings from their hold; and with the assistance of the baroness, unclosing the heavy door, they escaped without difficulty through the aperture; again covering the opening, they turned from the bandit's cave, and still guided by the blue flame, proceeded through the mazes of the forest.

The heavy clouds fleeting over the silvery moon, seemed gathering in the darksome atmosphere, portentous of an approaching storm; and soon large drops of rain rattled on the thick foliage of the trees; pale flashes of electric fire shot across the forest, succeeded by a low rumbling of distant thunder, yet the mystic flame, dimmed not by the falling rain, and quivering in the passing blast, preserved its steady light.

The baroness and Eglantine, enveloped more closely in the Banditti's cloaks, continued with a quick pace to follow their awful guide. The violence of the tempest increased: every moment the lightning became more forked and vivid; the tremendous peals of thunder echoed through the forest.

For nearly an hour, had they buffetted the warring elements, when, on emerging from the thicker part of the forest, a large building of gothic appearance arose upon their view. With redoubled speed, the rain-drenched fugitives followed the guiding flame; as with quickened flash it glided through the air towards the lonely edifice.

The baroness and Eglantine paused a moment, when they gained the draw-bridge, to survey with minute attention the exterior of the edifice. It was a large irregularly built castle, whose mouldering walls and fallen towers bore testimony of its antiquity, yet still, though a greater portion was sinking to decay, the part that remained habitable covered an immense space of ground.

The blue light had passed over the bridge, and stationing itself in a position to reflect its beams on a small postern that unfastened, waved to and fro, as if impelled by the wind.—For a moment, the fugitives hesitated reluctantly; but the superstitious awe with which the mysterious flame had inspired them, seemed to increase the more they looked at it; and the baroness, nearly exhausted by fatigue, anxiety, and her recent wound, resolved to avail herself of a shelter, till the subsiding of the storm should allow them again to proceed.—Leaning for support upon the arm of Eglantine, she passed through the opening into a small unfurnished chamber; and still conducted by the light, entered a long winding passage; at the end of which was an open door, leading to a number of stone stairs, formed in a spiral direction. The Lady Gertrude, unwilling to proceed, though the flame still hovered round the dark descent, remained for a while motionless on the topmost step; their supernatural guide slowly descended the wide opening, round which the spiral staircase wound; and soon its diminishing beam became nearly lost to the eyes of the Lady di Montalban and Eglantine, as, with anxious gaze they bent over the charm. "O! Eglantine, it is gone," exclaimed the baroness, "and whither now, lost to its guidance, shall we bend our weary steps."

"Enter, and fear not!" was pronounced in a voice, that, rising from beneath, sounded in sepulchral accent on the ear. As though impelled by some magnetic influence, the baroness arose; the light became visible, and she began to descend. Eglantine fearfully lingered; "Lady, you will not leave me?" she cried, as she caught the hand of the baroness within her own; "and I cannot—O! I dare not follow thee"

"Enter and fear not!" was the second time spoken

in the same hollow tone, and the Lady di Montalban again proceeded. All was now hushed in unbroken silence; and nearly involved in darkness, the trembling Eglantine, with faltering steps, accompanied her determined companion, and they together gained the vault in which the stairs ended; the light which had remained stationary during their descent, now moved towards a pannel, which partly sliding from its place, was discovered to the eyes of the baroness and Bandit's daughter. The Lady di Montalban enlarged the opening, and preceding Eglantine, entered a large spacious dungeon, of a most gloomy appearance, a wide slab of dark coloured stone, supported by four low pillars, stood nearly in the middle, which, with two seats of old fashioned structures, and a miserable pallet, comprised the furniture of the dreary apartment. Eglantine and the baroness approached the slab; their curiosity was excited, by perceiving something of a doubtful appearance laying upon it.

The blue flame had fixed itself at the head of the dusty coloured marble, and gradually lessening to their view, as the baroness, with an unsteady hand, removed the crimson cloak that covered the concealed object, it was in a few moments lost in a thick curling smoke. The hand of the Lady di Montalban still grasped the cloak, as she continued to gaze, with trembling anxiety, on the increasing vapour; suddenly it evaporated; unnumbered lights glittered around the walls of the dungeon; and the bleeding shade of Montalban's chieftain appeared to the fixed gaze of the agonized Gertrude. Three dismal groans re-echoed through the lofty dungeons! and the pale spirit, pointing to its earthly form that laid a murdered corpse upon the cold stone before it, gradually vanished from their sight! The baroness, uttering a piercing shriek, fell senseless to the ground!

A peal of awful thunder broke in a tremendous crash over the trembling ruin; and the dungeon became enveloped in impervious darkness. Eglantine, scarcely more conscious than the widowed lady of the ill-starred di Montalban, knelt by her side; resting her cold cheek upon her bosom, she endeavoured, by chafing her temples, to restore animation; but though she had continued her attempt for several minutes, no success smiled upon the effort; and Eglantine, unknowing where to seek acceptance, (even if alone, and in the dark, she could have found courage to explore the building,) strove to wait with patience the event, almost believing herself incapable of surviving the horrors of the night.

The tempest had ceased, and no sound, save the frequent sighs that issued from the hapless Eglantine, now broke on the awful stillness that prevailed around. With the most torturing apprehensions, the anxious maid continued her endeavours to revive the insensible baroness; at length, a faint respiration heaved the chilled bosom; the almost motionless pulse gradually regained their vibration; and a low imperfect sound murmured on the colourless lips —"Eglantine!" at length articulated the Lady Gertrude, in a more distinct accent, "Eglantine, I feel the hand of death weigh heavy at my heart; soon the vital spark will cease to burn, and this distracted brain will lose its agonized recollection. Leave me, my beloved child; let not the last moments of my existence be embittered by the consciousness that thou art left in a situation so horrible, a fate so doubtful. Arouse the fleeting energies of thy mind, and hasten to the more habitable part of the castle; perchance thou mayest discover inmates, who will sooth the awful moment of my dissolution with the wished for assurance of protecting thee."—"And leave thee!" Eglantine energetically exclaimed. "O! no,—no! if indeed thou must fall a victim to this fatal night, the wretched Eglantine will not survive thee." The baroness groaned heavily, she would have spoken, but faint from the exertion she had already made, she was unequal to the effort. Eglantine, terrified by the deathlike coldness, that stole over the form of the Lady di Montalban, and the dying langour by which she appeared oppressed, arose, and actuated by the first impulse, ran shrieking through the dungeon; hoping by her cries, to awake the slumbering inmates, if there were any in the desolate ruins.

As she grouped along the walls of the dungeon, her hand struck violently against the bolt of a small door, and hastily unclosed it; she perceived a lighted lamp laying on the ground; with eager haste she seized the welcome relief, and returned to the expiring baroness.

The Lady di Montalban, during her absence, had raised herself from the ground, and by a last effort of strength, had thrown herself on the low bier by the side of the breathless body of her murdered Lord. The bandage that bound her side had fallen in the attempt, and the stream of life was fast flowing from the re-opened wound. The cold dew of mortality stood on her livid forehead, and every feature bore the ghostly hue of death. Eglantine, with the most agonized emotions, took her clammy hand that hung lifeless over the dark stone, and sinking on her knees, called in accents of wildness and horror, on the name of the Lady di Montalban: the lustreless eyes of the baroness slowly unclosed, and as they rivetted their gaze on the kneeling Eglantine, the lips motioned to speak, but the power of articulation had for ever fled! the numbed hand strove to return the pressure of the trembling one, by which it was tenderly grasped; but exhausted nature forbade more than the silent farewell. A short convulsion seized her struggling form, her heavy eye lids closed, and with a long, and awful groan, the released spirit burst from its mortal frame.

Eglantine, with clasped hands and distended eye-balls, continued for several minutes to gaze in silent anguish on the lifeless form of her last and only friend. The sound of the turret clock striking the hour of four, aroused her from the stupor that had begun to creep over her senses, and starting from her intent gaze on the pale corpse of the baroness, she cast a timid glance around the dreary dungeon: taking up the lamp from the spot on which she had deposited it, she found the oil nearly exhausted, and timidly shrinking from a prospect of renewed darkness, resolved, assisted by its light, to quit the dread inspiring vault. With a view to discover whether the dungeon in which she had found the lamp, contained a flight of stairs that might lead her by a nearer route into the centre of the building, than that by which she had entered, she proceeded towards the little door, but ere she gained it, it was unclosed by another hand, and a dark, tall figure stood before her! one thin emaciated hand held a lamp, correspondent to that she had found, and in the other was upraised a drawn sabre, whose hilt of polished brightness glittered in the rays of the light, but whose point was deeply stained by human blood. A harsh severity sat on each gloomy feature, and the large black eyes were bent with penetrating scrutiny on the beauteous countenance of the bandit's daughter. The stranger advanced, and Eglantine, fearful of his approach, attempted by flight to elude his pursuit; but her trembling limbs refused their support; she lost her senses, and with a faint cry, fell into the arms of him she was seeking to escape.

The insensibility of Eglantine was but momentary, and on opening her eyes, she found some one was lightly bearing her through a considerable part of the building, and the heavy footfalls of another were following the steps of the one in whose arms she was carried :—not daring to trust herself with a glance at the countenance of her companions, fearful of encountering the stern gaze she had recoiled at, she suffered herself to be borne a passive burthen.—In a few minutes, they gained a corridor, at the top of the first flight of the grand stairs, and one of the men, unclosing a door she was carried by the other into an elegant and spacious saloon; he who bore the lamp, now lit a wax light that stood on the table, and then quitted the room. Eglantine, without daring to raise her eyes, had, in the interim, been placed by him who had supported her, on a couch of crimson velvet, embroidered with gold. The hand of the stranger was gently pressed upon her heart, to discover if aught of palpitation remained, whilst a voice of manly firmness, yet of softest melody, addressed her in the tenderest accents of kind solicitude;—the sensitive heart of the sweet maid swelled with emotions of gratitude, and no longer fearful of beholding the countenance of a being whose feelings appeared so kindly compassionate, she raised her soft blue eyes to those of the stranger. Eglantine was not deceived in the expectancy she had formed; the eyes that met her's, blended the fire and vivacity of youth, with the softer beams of heavenly sensibility—the richest glow of health vermillioned the sun-burnt cheek, partially shaded by a profusion of ebon tresses, that wantoned in careless ringlets over the high-arched forehead—grace and intelligence marked each expressive feature, and the elegance of superior rank characterized his well proportioned and warlike figure.

Eglantine was about to satisfy the enquiries of Adelbert, by giving him a detail of her little history, when the door of the saloon unclosed, and the elder stranger entered, and was introduced by the younger as his uncle, the Baron di Rosini. The baron approached the couch, as Adelbert announced him to their unknown guest; but no sooner had his eye rested on the sweet Eglantine, than the blood forsook his lips, his cheeks assumed a livid hue, and, with a heavy groan, he would have fallen senseless to the ground, had not the ready arm of his nephew caught him. The restoratives that had been applied to Eglantine, were now offered the Signior di Rosini, and in a few minutes animation was restored.

The baron, on recovery, waved his hand for the domestic who had followed him into the saloon, to return; and re-approaching Eglantine, with one hand he grasped her arm, whilst with the other he held to his view a miniature that had escaped the concealment of her vest, and demanded, in accents of authoritative sternness and agitating emotion, by what means it came into her possession? Eglantine, timidly shrinking from the penetrating eye that pursued her, informed the baron, that the picture he was then contemplating was the resemblance of her mother, and that on the other side was the likeness of her father in his early youth. The tremor that at first agitated the frame of the Signior di Rosini, became so strong as Eglantine replied to his enquiries, that he was necessitated to lean upon Adelbert for support; and when he was sufficiently restored to composure, as to be able to articulate, he called upon Eglantine as his daughter! the beloved image of his sainted Constance; and, kneeling by the couch, pressed her in wild extacy to his heart.

Adelbert now fully comprehended the meaning of the baron's emotion, and fearful for the event both on his aged relative and the suffering Eglantine, he endeavoured to calm the mind of his uncle, entreating him to defer explanation till the coming morn; alleging, the weak state of the harassed maid, rendered the quiet of repose necessary previous to any new trial. The Signior di Rosini, submitted to the suggestions of Adelbert; and Bianca, the domestic, who had been summoned from her pallet, was called into the room, and Eglantine was given to her charge, with orders to conduct her to her apartment, and watch her while she slept. Tenderly supported by the Count Adelbert, the bandit's daughter ascended the turret stairs that led to the chamber of Bianca, at the door of which, he left her to the care of her attendant, and then rejoined the baron.

Fair and guileless was Constance, the daughter of the Baron di Rosini; health and beauty graced her youthful mein, and the sportive playfulness of unchecked gaiety frolicked in each lovely feature. The early loss of a wife whom he tenderly loved, had occasioned the baron to have a distate for the pleasures of the world, and engendered a propensity to solitude that appeared almost natural; death had deprived him of every relative to whom his heart had been attached; and no longer desirous of mixing with the world, (saving when his duty as a soldier called him from the retirement of his castle,) he spent each leisure hour within its sequestered walls. Reared within the gloomy shades of Sebastine, the blooming Constance attained the age of seventeen; her only companions (excepting a few casual guests) were her governess the Signiora Viola, and Jacquelina, a humble friend, of nearly her own age. The widowed heart of the Baron di Rosini felt its every wish, its every emotion of affection, centered in his child; and he watched, with unceasing care and fond delight, the maturing beauties of her person, and the strengthening virtues of her mind.

The frequent hostilities in which his country was engaged, now often called him from his solitude of St. Sebastine; and it was in one of those absences that the beauty of the lady Constance first met the eye of the bandit of the forest. The Signior Roderigo encountered the lovely fair in one of her rambles from the castle of her sire; and deeply interested by the captivating loveliness of her person, he sought again to behold her.—Constance, hitherto secluded from the admiring gaze of youthful cavaliers, felt herself no less pleased with the manly person of the handsome chieftain; and eagerly continued her accustomed walks;—often they met, and the bandit at length venturing to address her, stole, by degrees, on her unsuspecting nature; and Constance, in the innocent confidence of her heart, yielded to him its best affections, convinced by the sophistry of his arguments, that no real impropriety could be attached to their clandestine intercourse.

At length but a fortnight was wanting to the return of the baron; when one morn, as Constance hastened to meet her lover, she found him labouring under the appearance of the deepest distress. Anxiously she enquired the cause;—the crafty Roderigo informed her, that a hasty summons to rejoin his father, at the seat of his progenitors, for the purpose of espousing a lady who had been destined by his parents for his bride, must hasten his departure far from the beloved shades of Sebastine.—Yet Heaven knows, added the bandit, my heart, fondly wedded to its beloved Constance, will never acknowledge a second mistress! no! beauteous maid, though I dare not hope to be considered by the Baron di Rosini as his son, from the enmity that has existed between his family and my own, never will I espouse the daughter of another.

Constance, subdued by the emotion that swelled in her bosom, leaned her aching head upon the shoulder of the bandit as she listened to the torturing intelligence, that told her they must part. Roderigo perceived the conflict that agitated her mind, and anxious to avail himself of the discovery, he again spoke of the animosity that subsisted between the house of Rosini and his own, urging that as a motive for concealing the name of the latter, and finally pleading for a private marriage, encouraged her to rely on the affection of her father for forgiveness, when it should be made known; concluding, by avowing an intention, should she refuse, of for ever banishing himself from her sight. Constance found her fears of the baron's anger too weak to combat her inclination: the Signior Roderigo obtained her consent to his wishes, and on the ensuing night their vows were in private sanctioned by a father from the adjacent convent.

Several months elapsed, after the return of the baron, ere Constance, urged by her fears of detection, revealed to him the act of filial disobedience of which she had been guilty.—Jacquelina had already been apprised of it, and the bandit would long before have removed his sweet bride to the immuring gloom of his subterraneous habitation had not the charms of Jacquelina begun to rival, in his faithless heart, the image of the lady Constance. The baron's interest in the happiness of his child, and the affection he bore her, soon became ascendant over the feelings of resentment that had at first kindled in his bosom;—he desired to behold the Signior Roderigo, and after pronouncing his pardon he demanded the name of the family of which he was a member. The bandit hesitated; he entreated time, ere he ventured to satisfy the enquiries of di Rosini, at the same time assuring him, that the motives by which he was influenced in making the request, he doubted not would meet with his approbation.

At the beginning of the following week, the Lady Constance gave birth to a daughter who, at the request of the baron, was christened by the name of Eglantine, after the ever lamented Baroness di Rosini.—Constance, happy in the forgiveness of her sire, in the apparent tenderness of her lord, was soon sufficiently recovered to leave her chamber; the little babe flourished in health and beauty under her care, and the sunshine of joy seemed to diffuse its bright beams over the inmates of St. Sebastine. But, alas! a heavy cloud, fraught with calamity, soon overspread the prospect; the Signior Roderigo, on the day preceding that in which he had promised to reveal his name, disappeared from the castle; and with him, Jacquelina and the infant Eglantine; and though, for several months the strictest search was made after them, not the slightest vestige could be discovered.

The bandit, aware of his inability to reply to the enquiries of the baron, and no longer retaining a spark of affection for the deserted Constance, had alone been waiting a favourable opportunity for conveying Jacquelina, the second object of his attachment, from the castle.—The day on which they had been supposed voluntarily to have migrated from St. Sebas tine, Jacquelina had, with the infant Eglantine, wandered unaccompanied to the recesses of the forest; and, entering a thickly embowered shade, had been seized by the watchful emissaries of Roderigo, and conveyed to the cave, where, in an interview with the Signior, he unfolded the full baseness of his character. Several attempts to escape were mad by Jacquelina without success; and she at length (wholly discouraged by the fruitlessness of her efforts.) yielded herself a passive victim to her fate. The little Eglantine was the only consolation of which her mind was sensible; and intimidated by the threat of the bandit to deprive her of her infant solace in case of refusal she vowed, in a manner the most solemn, to comply with his desire, in permitting Eglantine to remain wholly ignorant of her birth—of the world—and the means by which the society of the cave were supported.

Often did Jacquelina as she gazed on the innocent countenance of the bandit's daughter, feel half tempted to break through the awful promise she had made; but her better reason, as it pointed out the evil of which it might be productive, and but the slight chance of benefit, checked the desire; and even when Eglantine discovered the secret opening, she determined not to infringe on her vow, conscious that her debility (for it was in the last days of an illness that terminated her existence.) would not permit her to accompany her flight, and she feared for the danger that might attend the escape of a being so inexperienced—so unknown, had she attempted it by herself.

Meanwhile, the helpless, deserted Constance became a martyr to her ill requited affection for the faithless Roderigo; a violent fever, occasioned by the agitation of her mind, left her debilitated in constitution, and shattered in intellect. No feelings of anguish could exceed the poignancy of those that tortured the lacerated bosom of the baron, as he gazed on the faded loveliness of her person, and listened to the wild accents of distress that fell from his insane, his blighted Constance—oft as he watched the burning tears that rolled down her pallid cheek, would he breathe vows of determined vengeance against their ruthless cause, should some future period discover his retreat.

Every means were fruitlessly exerted to restore the wandering reason of the Lady Constance; her mind still harped upon her friend, her lover, and her child; and discovering in a chamber contiguous to her own, a sabre, that had for many years lain concealed amongst a heap of lumber, the idea of suicide suggested itself to her distracted brain. Not long did Constance wait an opportunity of accomplishing her purpose; her attendants, unsuspicious of danger, not unfrequently left her to herself, and in the first moment that she found herself alone, the poor maniac plunged the fatal weapon into her breaking heart.

No language can do justice to the agony of the baron, when informed of the event by one of the domestics who had discovered the bleeding body of the self murdered Constance; for several hours he raved in all the wildness of unbounded sorrow; and, when more composed, he was permitted to visit the pale corpse, he swore in a manner the most solemn. as he held the blood-stained weapon in his hand, to avenge his own and the wrongs of his Constance on the guilty bandit. "Never! never!" pursued the baron, as he fixed his eyes upon the fatal instrument, "never shall the crimson die be obliterated from thy point! no, my beloved child, my soul's last treasure, the accursed steel that has robbed thee of existence, (still imbrued in the vital stream that circled round thy heart,) shall be plunged into the remorseless breast of thy undoer." The baron had never since permitted the sabre to leave his own apartment, save, when often in the dead of the night he visited the tomb of the murdered Constance.—It was on one of those nights, that a domestic of the Lady Gertrude, who had escaped the prey of the banditti, and had hastened to acquaint his lord of the fatal catastrophe, guided the steps of the still invalid Baron di Montalban to the forest (who. well mounted, had lost no time in hastening to the succour of the Baroness), but, being met by a party of the ferocious crew, the brave di Montalban fell a lifeless victim to their desire of plunder, and the attendants who had accompanied him became captives to the robbers. Scarcely had they begun to move from the scene of action, ere the sound of many horses in approach alarmed them for their safety; but, turning from the direction that led to the cave, they hastened to the vaults of St Sebastine; and depositing the murdered form of the baron on a stone slab, they at length ventured again into the forest, leaving the body behind them.

The sire of Constance, on those nights that he repaired to the dungeon in which was deposited the cold remains of his child, usually furnished himself with two lamps, for the purpose of rescuing himself from the evil consequences that might attend the extinguishment of one, in case of his not being provided with a second.—The wild cries of Eglantine, in the last moments of the unfortunate baroness, reached the ear of di Rosini, and fearful of entering the dungeon from whence the sound proceeded, unaccompanied; (leaving one of his lights in the next vault), he repaired with the other to the chamber of Adelbert, and they together returned.

The mind of Eglantine was too greatly agitated by the variety of strange and distressing incidents that had occurred during the last few hours. to allow her, for a considerable time, to close her eyes in sleep; and when at length, wearied by the fatigues she had undergone, a short slumber stole o'er her harassed spirits, the vision it presented was so replete with objects of terror, that starting, she awoke. At an early hour, Adelbert presented himself at the door of Bianca's chamber, with an anxious enquiry after the interesting charge. The reply of Bianca was far from satisfactory; and the baron, alarmed at the account he received from Adelbert, repaired to the apartment. Eglantine no longer shrank from the gaze of di Rosini; his countenance had lost the gloom and moroseness that had before impressed it; and melancholy and tenderness were now its most striking expressions.

The Signior beheld with alarm the hectic flush that had arisen on her cheek, and the pious father who acted as confessor, and occasionally as physician, to the baron, was summoned to attend her. Eglantine, under the assiduous care of the friends by whom she was surrounded, was soon sufficiently recovered from the effects of the slight fever, that had resulted from the terror and chill she had encountered on the night of her escape. The remains of the Baron and Baroness di Montalban had, during her illness, been sent by the Signior di Rosini, to be interred in the tomb of their ancestors; accompanied by a trusty messenger, who undertook to break the mournful intelligence to the relatives of the deceased.

Eglantine, soon as her spirits had sufficiently recovered to bear the agitating recital, had been informed by the baron of the hapless fate of her mother, and as much of the history of her paternal parent, as had reached the knowledge of the Signior. Di Rosini, fearful of awakening her fears for the safety of her father, should he first enter on an explanation, had previously drawn from Eglantine the little narrative of her own life; trusting by that means to discover in what sequestered spot the Signior Roderigo had secreted himself. The simple narrator, unacquainted with the necessity of concealing from the knowledge of a being, apparently so kind, the smallest incident, revealed, without disguise, the persuasions which the Baroness di Montalban had exerted, in prevailing on her to quit the cave. The baron, as he listened to the tale, was no longer ignorant of the motives which had influenced the conduct of the bandit; and entering on the detail of her own sorrows, and those of the Lady Constance, he sought to impress more deeply on her mind the lesson which the Baroness di Montalban had begun.

The quick comprehension of Eglantine soon became fully sensible of the guilty course pursued by her sire and his abandoned crew; yet her merciful nature shrank from the plan of vengeance which di Rosini imparted; and though she had not described the actual spot, (for she knew not in what part of the forest it was situated), yet she trembled, lest she had already said too much for the baron to miss the discoverv; her benevolent heart, refusing conviction to the arguments of di Rosini, tended to impress her with a sense of the justice of the revenge he meditated. Though she had never felt for the harsh Signior Roderigo the affections of a child, yet she remembered he was her father; and, considering him in that light, she could not for a moment, without horror, think of the bloody purpose of the baron; and that, probably through her, he might be discovered to the unappeased hatred and power of di Rosini. Eglantine, kneeling at the feet of the determined baron, pleaded with all the eloquence of nature's feeling for the devoted Roderigo; but his injured enemy, firm to his purpose, listened unmoved to her supplications; and commanding her in a tone of severity, never again to offend his ears with entreaties to spare the detested bandit the fate he merited, quitted her presence.

Eglantine had not again ventured to implore the mercy of the Baron; and di Rosini, pleased with her forbearance, treated her with the tender indulgence of an affectionate parent; and reluctant to give her unnecessary pain, had, without imparting to her his intention, dispatched notice to the court of the knowledge he had obtained of the bandit's habitation. A party of soldiers were immediately sent to search the forest; the scrutiny was successful, and all the desperadoes, excepting the chieftain, (whose absence at the time secured his safety,) were borne triumphant from their long undiscovered place of rendezvous.

Meanwhile Eglantine, ignorant of the event, and hoping from the manner of the baron, and his remaining inactive at the castle, that he had forgone his purpose, gradually regained her spirits:—the truant roses rebloomed upon her cheek, the lustre which illness had dimmed, again sparkled in her eye, and smiles of innocence and delight played round her ruby lips. Already had the noble heart of the gallant Adelbert paid homage to the modest graces of her person, and the guileless purity of her mind; nor had Eglantine beheld the manly deportment, the brilliant talents, and the virtues that adorned the character of the young warrior, with a slight degree of interest:—together they would ramble through the romantic scenery that environed St. Sebastine; and often, when the summer sun sank beneath the western horizon, they would watch from the battlements of the castle its departing rays.—" How serenely beautiful is this view," observed Adelbert to his fair companion, as they one evening watched the gradual decline of the glorious luminary; " how welcome to the sight of the labourer are its farewell beams. See, sweetest Eglantine, where yonder peasant hastens o'er the grassy soil; he bounds with a buoyant step that partakes not of fatigue."—" And yet he must be very weary," said Eglantine. " True," returned Adelbert, " for he has toiled through the day; but you observe not the little family that hastens to greet his return; he has a bride who meets him with a smile, and prattling cherubs, that tipping lightly o'er the sod, cling round his knees, and, lisping accents of unaffected joy, lead him to his peaceful habitation; his heart dilates with happiness and gratitude, that gives an elasticity to his frame, and he no longer feels the lassitude of fatigue. O, Eglantine! how happy, how enviable is yon humble swain: rich in the tenderness of her he loves, he covets not the luxuries of golden wealth.

" Surely he is not happier than you, my lord," said Eglantine, " have you not friends, by whom you are as tenderly beloved? and do you not possess the means of procuring all the comforts of existence, without the necessity of toil!"—" Not all, sweet Eglantine," returned Adelbert: " alas! I fear the good I covet—the blessing that can alone give value to those that are already in my power, is too far beyond my merit, to allow a hope of its attainment."

" I should be very, very sorry, if indeed it were so!" said Eglantine, with an innocent earnestness. " You would pity me then, dear angelic maid," exclaimed Adelbert, " and if it were in your power, you would bestow on me the blessing so fervently desired?" " O yes, indeed I would," returned Eglantine. " and it would make me happy!"

Adelbert pressed the soft hand he had taken with fervency

to his lips. "Dear, dear Eglantine! is it you, and you only, who can bestow that felicity, that, till within these few weeks, I felt not the desire of possessing."—"But tell me what you wish dear Adelbert?" said Eglantine. "I am sure, if I can make you happy, you shall not long be otherwise. "I scarcely dare to name the boon I solicit," exclaimed Adelbert, sinking on one knee. "O! Eglantine, how shall I presume to tell thee, that I aspire to the possession of a being as transcendently lovely in person, so inestimably valuable in mind and heart, as the angelic daughter of the sainted Constance; yes, Eglantine, the resistless influence of thy attractions have stolen with a power over my heart, that every effort (did I wish to break the sweet enchantment,) would be ineffectual to subdue; thy image, if absent from my sight, is ever present to my fancy—my dreams are delightful, for Eglantine is their object;—the heavy gloom that prevailed through the lofty chambers of St. Sebastine has dispersed; and the dull solitude by which it was surrounded, and which appeared so intolerable, is now no longer irksome; for the sweet voice of Eglantine, vibrating through the ancient edifice, breathes cheerfulness and pleasure within its lonely walls; and her sportive form, bounding through the dreary mazes of the forest, or tripping lightly o'er the barren heaths, seems to impart a genial animation to the dullest scenes."

The Count paused, and Eglantine, silent and blushing, hung her head.—"Alas! you do not reply to me!" at length he articulated. "Adelbert is not dear to the heart of Eglantine; and her gentle nature shrinks from confirming the dreadful suspicion."—"O! think not thus unkindly of me," said Eglantine, raising her soft eyes to those of her lover; "I am not indeed I am not so ungrateful." Adelbert read in the expressive beaming of her eye, the tenderness impressed on her artless countenance, a confirmation of his every wish; and again addressing her, he drew from the guileless fair one a tender assurance of mutual regard.

The shades of night had thickened around, ere they thought of returning to the castle; the baron expressed surprise, as they entered, at the length of their absence; and Adelbert, soon after the evening's repast was removed, requesting a private audience, unfolded to him the passion which himself and Eglantine had mutually imbibed. Di Rosini listened with evident satisfaction to the communication of the Count, and on his concluding, he expressed in warm terms the pleasure it afforded him, yielding at the same time a free concurrence to the union, when his plan of destroying the banditti should be finally accomplished. Meanwhile, a rumour had reached the ears of the household of the castle, of the fate of the robbers; and the baron, fearful it could not much longer remain a secret to Eglantine, and unwilling that it should be communicated in an abrupt manner, undertook to be himself her informant. Eglantine listened with the deepest interest to the detail; she shuddered as he pourtrayed the fate of the beings with whom from infancy she had associated; and though she dared not openly to evince the satisfaction she felt, she was truly rejoiced, that the chief of the band had escaped the ignominious punishment which the others had suffered.

The strictest search was now made, by order of the magistrates, after the Signior Roderigo; large rewards were offered not only by the police, but by his implacable enemy, the baron. Eglantine waited the event, with an anxiety, that rendered her nearly callous to the delights which the society of St. Sebastine had before imparted;—the roses gradually became fainter on her cheek, and the sparkling animation faded from her eye. Adelbert beheld, with the deepest concern, the distressing alteration; he knew the cause; but, at the same time, he was too well acquainted with the inflexibity of the Signor di Rosini, to implant a hope in the mind of Eglantine, of relinquishing his long-cherished purpose of revenge.

The solicitude felt by the bandit's daughter for the fate of her sire, frequently stole from her bewildered senses the sweet composure of sleep.—One evening more than usually agitated, she retired to her chamber, for the morning had brought intelligence of the bandit having been recognized in a small village, from which, however, he had fled without being taken; the information concluded, by saying, he had been almost immediately followed in the direction he had been seen to pursue.

Eglantine felt no inclination to sleep; and unwilling to retire, for some minutes she continued to pace to and fro; fearful images arose in succession on her mind—the murdered form of Montalban's chief—the ill-fated baroness—and the horrors they had encountered on the night of her escape from the cave, were alternately dwelt upon; and conspiring with the melancholy stillness of the night, and the gloomy appearances of her chamber, threw a fearful dread over her spirits, that made her start at the echo of her steps, and timidly shrink from the shadow of her own form reflected in the mirrors, situated in different parts of the gothic room. Eglantine, unable to shake off the increasing sensation of terror which had impressed her imagination, beheld with dismay the exhausted oil of her lamp, that threatened in a short time to leave her in all the horrors of darkness: unable to sustain with resolution, an anticipation so distressing in her present frame of mind, she resolved to hasten to Bianca's chamber, and rather to impart to her the weakness she could not overcome, than to pass the remainder of the tedious night without light, and probably without sleep.

Eglantine taking her lamp, she opened a small door leading by a back way to Bianca's apartment, less circuitous than that in general pursued; she passed through a long gallery winding round the tower, and ascending a few steps at its termination, she found herself on a small landing-place on which there were two chambers; the door of each was made so exactly alike, that Eglantine, but imperfectly acquainted with the route she was to pursue, hesitated which to unclose; opening one, she entered a small circular room, in which were a number of statues ranged around; she passed towards the further end, but soon discovered she had mistaken the apartment, since it contained no outlet whatever, but the door by which she had entered.

Eglantine turned to leave the chamber with an intention of entering the other, and casting a timid glance at the statues, that stood on either side of the door in the attitude of guarding it, had gained the opening, when the out-streached hand of one of the figures caught her in its firm grasp; the body moved slowly from its station, and whilst with one arm it encircled the shrieking form of Eglantine, with the hand of the other it drew the beaver from his face, and the eye of the bandit's daughter rested on the stern countenance of her sire!

Eglantine, uttering a shriek of terror, fell senseless in the arms of the Signior Roderigo; when she revived, she found herself reclining on a bed, in a chamber contiguous to her own; the bandit, with a taper in one hand, and a sabre in the other, standing over her; an expression of fear, mingled with the fire of resentment, shot from his large dark eyes, as they rested on the pale features of the trembling Eglantine. "This is no time," exclaimed the bandit, as he rudely shook the arm of his daughter; "this is no time," he repeated, in a harsher accent, "to yield to feminine weakness; every moment of delay may prove fatal to my safety—even now the emissaries of revenge may have traced me to this hated building, and the devoted Roderigo, in the presence of his unpitying child, fall a sacrifice to her unnatural, inhuman conduct."

"Oh! forbear this cruel, this unmerited upbraiding," exclaimed the half-distracted Eglantine. "Heaven knows that I would sooner, far sooner, sacrifice my own existence, than betray thus my unhappy, my persecuted sire, to the direful purpose of the Signior di Rosini."

"Dissembler!" cried the bandit vehemently, "hast thou not already betrayed me to the sanguinary di Rosini? Hast thou not already pointed out the secret of the cave, and gloried in the destruction of my brave associates?"—"Oh! never, never," exclaimed Eglantine; "the Baron di Rosini, unknown to me, discovered thy retreat; I did not glory, no! whilst I shrunk with horror at the history of their guilt, I wept for the sufferings of thy unhappy band; and though I fear it is alas! too true, that through my undisguised narration on the night of my escape, the long-concealed cavern was discovered, yet, when aware of the danger attending revealment, I refused further to satisfy the enquiries of the baron; and never, till within these two weeks, did I know of the measures that had been taken; and since thus alarmed for thy fate, I have been lost to enjoyment; the pleasures of the day have fled, and my nights have been spent in restless uneasiness."

"Beware of falsehood!" replied the bandit: "know that Roderigo, though so apparently powerless, has still the means of vengeance within his possession; and thou, Eglantine, will do well to remember, that those who offend him, offend not with impunity.—It is true, that I feel inclined to credit the assertion thou hast made; yet, I cannot be satisfied, unless by vow the most solemn, thou shalt attest the sincerity of thy declaration." Eglantine, with an earnestness of manner that spoke conviction to the mind of the bandit, professed herself ready to affirm by the oath designed by the Seignior, (however awful in its import,) the truth of what she had alleged, and sinking on her knees, she repeated, in distinct accents the attestations required.

"Now, Eglantine!" said the bandit, in an imperious tone, as he raised her from the ground, "give me thy most serious attention; satisfied with the solemn assurance thou hast uttered, I am about to repose in thee a trust, which every tie of nature, of religion, enjoins thee to observe;—to thy disposal I commit my safety; the number of those employed in pursuit of me, and the clue they have obtained in the search, no longer allows me a hope of eluding them by flight; in the forest, is a small subterraneous dwelling, known but to myself; the late chieftain of our ill-starred association confided to my knowledge the secret of its situation, avowing at the same time, that to me alone he had unfolded it. Thither will I repair; and since its vicinity to the castle will render my leaving it, even in the solemn hour of midnight, attendant with peril, thou, Eglantine, once a week, at an hour past midnight, must repair to my lonely refuge with a sufficiency of food to support me in the intermediate time; promise then, my child, should thy kindly intent be by some unhappy chance suspected, that thou wilt buffet the threats, the utmost malice of di Rosini, rather than violate the trust reposed in thee."

"I do promise most faithfully, most sacredly," said Eglantine, as she again sank on her knees. "I am satisfied," said the bandit in a low tone; "now follow me." Eglantine arose, and, in obedience to the desire of the bandit, in silence persued his steps. Soon they gained the buttery of the castle; and Eglantine, taking from thence a small supply of viands, and a flask of homely wine, which was allowed as a beverage for the servants, passed with the bandit to a small door, opening into a court-yard: Signior Roderigo hastened to undo the numerous fastening by which the door was secured, when a noise, like a footstep in advance, filled him with alarm, and hastened to unclose the portal, in the hurry and agitation of the moment, an iron bar slipt from his hand, and fell with a loud sound upon the floor,—uttering a tremendous oath, he darted through the opening, followed by the faltering steps of Eglantine; gaining the opposite side of the court-yard, he found the gate too strongly fastened to admit a hope of unloosing them, and turning from them with renewed speed, he hastened round the walls towards a distant part, in which was situated the door by which he had entered. Eglantine, swift as the terror that shook her frame would permit, followed the steps of the bandit, but ere she could reach him, a tall figure, wrapt in a loose robe, glided between, which the Signior Roderigo no sooner perceived, than bounding forward he became in a moment lost to her view. The object he was seeking to fly, for a few paces pursued him, but quickly returning, he overtook Eglantine ere she had time to retire; and the ray of her light reflecting on his face, she discovered the Baron di Rosini.

"Eglantine!" demanded the Signior, in an authoritative tone, "how comest thou here? and who is the man with whom thou hast, at this late hour, been wandering through the castle?" Eglantine hesitated to reply; her pure ingenuous mind was incapable of subterfuge, and every consideration urged the concealment of the truth. "I cannot suspect," pursued the baron, after a pause, "that thou, who hast so lately plighted vows of fidelity and love to the Count Adelbert wouldst feel inclined to encourage the pretentions of a second suitor; there is an air of mystery in this affair, that gives birth to various suspicions that must, that shall be satsified: speak then, Eglantine, tell me the name of him with whom you have just parted."

"Oh! pray, do not ask me," said Eglantine, imploringly; "Indeed, my lord, I cannot, I must not tell you." "And why?" demanded the baron; "I insist, I command you by the authority of my age, my relationship, gives me,—by your duty as a child and dependant, I expect instant obedience." "Oh! my lord," said the distressed Eglantine, "did you but know the motives of my silence, I am very sure you would no longer entreat me to break through a bond so sacred, so indissoluble, as that which commands me to be secret." "Unhappy mistaken girl," said the baron, "thou hast said enough to confirm the suspicion arisen in my heart; the man, to preserve whose safety thou hast had the temerity to hazard my just resentment, is the villain Roderigo; the accursed destroyer of my child, my beloved Constance."

Eglantine was silent; a consciousness of the truth of the baron's surmise, and her inability to confute it, combining with the fear of her father's safety, and apprehension of di Rosini's anger with herself, created the agonizing embarrassment that prevented the power of utterance. The baron now rung an alarm that quickly summoned them instantly to prepare for pursuit; he again turned to Eglantine, and commanded her, on peril of incurring his everlasting displeasure, to discover what she knew of the route taken by the bandit.

With truth did Eglantine avow herself ignorant of the desired information, and the Signior di Rosini bidding her to retire, repaired to his own chamber to accoutre himself for the search, which he determined to lead. Eglantine, with a sad forboding of evil, heard the departure of the resolute di Rosini and his domestics, and throwing herself upon the couch, endeavoured to lull the torturing anxiety that filled her bosom, in the oblivion of sleep; but vainly did she try to compose her agitated spirits; the tedious night wore away without bringing even a temporary oblivion to the wakeful fair. At the first dawn of reviving morn, she arose from her pallet, and descended to the breakfast-room; the baron had a few minutes previous returned from his fruitless pursuit, and too irrirated in feeling, from his disappointment, to seek society, had ordered refreshment to be brought him in his own apartment.

Adelbert, to whom the Signior di Rosini imparted the events of the night, alternately endeavoured to extenuate to him the conduct of Eglantine, and to speak consolation to the saddened heart of the lovely maid not the slightest intimation passed his lips indicative of a desire to penetrate into the mystery of the Signior Roderigo venturing to enter the walls of St. Sebastine, and the motive of Eglantine's evident intention of accompanying him from the castle;—the count alone hinted, in terms too delicate to excite resentment in her gentle bosom, the fear he had imbibed, lest some artful persuasion of her sire should have induced her to think of abandoning her present habitation for one, in which he might never again taste the felicity of beholding her; and, satisfied with her assurance to the contrary, he waved a subject which he feared would give her pain.

The melancholy day was at length terminated, and Eglantine once more bent her steps towards her chamber; the image of her father, suffering the torture of extreme hunger, arose upon her mind; and determined her, at the hour prescribed by Roderigo for her nightly visits, to venture into the forest with a supply of food; in the hope of discovering, by some means, the spot he had selected as a refuge. She felt the extreme improbability of success, but the native benevolence of her disposition urged her too strongly to allow her to hesitate.

Supposing the domestics of the castle, weary from the fatigue of the preceding night, had early retired to rest, Eglantine felt more confident of her escaping detection; and as the clock struck one, she quitted her apartment, and repaired to the spot, from which she had before taken the viands, the bandit had left. Quickly she filled a basket, in which she had been wont to deposit her embroidery, and cautiously unclosing the door through which she had passed with her father, she hastened towards the small gate by which she had been admitted; she found it unfastened, and entered the forest, paused a moment to listen, if all remained quiet. The night was uncommonly still; the stars twinkled with sparkling lustre in a cloudless sky, and the bright beams of the full moon shone with refulgence on every object.

Eglantine, too much interested in the mission to feel fatigue, continued unwearied to persevere; bending at frequent intervals to the ground, and applying her lips to the green sod, she called as loudly as she dared on the name of Roderigo. Almost despairing of success, she had nearly given up the pursuit, when her steps unconsciously wandered towards the concealment of the bandit.

The Signior Roderigo, spent with hunger, and shrinking from the prospect of a death so horrible as that which threatened him, ventured towards the mouth of the cave, half tempted to brave the dangers of discovery, rather than submit to an alternative that appeared so inevitable; partially he raised the artfully-contrived door, that concealed the entrance of his retreat; he glanced a timid look around him, and catching a glimpse of the white garments of Eglantine, he fearfully closed the trap, but not till the beams of the moon had discovered it to his anxious child. With renovated strength and spirit, she gained the spot; soon her well-known voice reached the ear of the bandit, and admitting her to the dreary recess, he greedily partook of the provisions she had brought.—Eglantine, after a brief explanation, arose to depart; and taking the emtied basked in her hand, she quitted the cave and returned to the castle,

The Baron di Rosini, on the preceding night, had heard the shriek of Eglantine on her discovering the Signior Roderigo; and uncertain whence it proceeded, he first hastened to the chamber of the bandit's daughter, and finding it vacated, he hurried through several apartments and galleries, scarcely knowing whither; when the sound, occasioned by the falling of the iron-bar, conducted him to the spot from whence it issued.—Too much agitated to obtain repose on the ensuing eve, he seated himself in his chamber, and soon became absorbed in a continuance of the reflections that had engrossed him during the day. In spite of Eglantine's assurance, he felt inclined to believe she had deceived him, with regard to her professed ignorance of the bandit's plan of retreat; and the idea that suggested itself. from various surmises, of the Signior Roderigo seeking a second interview on the present night, determined him to, in part at least, satisfy his doubts, by repairing to the chamber of Eglantine, in order to ascertain if she remained within it; the hour was past that in which the bandit's daughter had quitted her chamber, and the baron, finding no answer returned to his frequent knocking, hastened towards the portal, by which the Signior Roderigo had quitted the castle on the foregoing night, and was soon convinced by the fastenings being removed, that she was no longer within the walls of St. Sebastine: and reparing to the lesser gate, he stationed himself on the inner side, impressed with a belief that she would return. At length, Eglantine reached the inclosure of the castle, and was lightly passing towards the interior building, when the Baron di Rosini presented himself to her startled view; deprived of motion by terror and surprise, for some moments she stood silent and irresolute before him;—the basket she held in her hand, brought with it the recollection of the one, which he had observed on the proceeding night, and the motive of Eglantine's nocturnal excursions rushed with conviction on his mind; yet vainly did the baron seek, by alternative threats and entreaties, to gain a knowledge of the bandit's concealment; firm to her trust, she resolutely refused compliance with the reiterated demand; and di Rosini at length, weary of his fruitless importunities, permitted her to retire, promising within himself to renew the endeavour the ensuing day.

Exhausted from the fatigue she had suffered on the present night, and her entire deprivation of rest on the foregoing. Eglantine soon lost the recollection of her distress in a tranquil sleep. from which she did not awake till a late hour. On unclosing her eyes, she found Bianca watching by her side, and replying to the kind enquiries of the aged attendant, by informing her, that she felt considerably refreshed, the latter quitted the room.—The Baron di Rosini, though so immovably resolved on his long projected purpose of revenge, yet felt for the situation of Eglantine;—the naturally vindictive bent of his disposition had been strengthened by education. and as he reflected on his oft-repeated vows of vengance, he regarded its fulfilment not only as an atonement to his injured feelings, but as a religious duty; he admired the firmness of Eglantine, because he doubted not the purity of the motive; though at the same time, his own principles allowed him no hesitation in believing the inducement to be a mistaken one; in this persuasion, he resolved, by every argument he could suggest. on endavouring to convince her of what he could not believe to be otherwise than a false notion of duty and integrity; and in case of failing in this endeavour, he determined, if possible, to terrify her into compliance, by placing her own happiness in competition with her interest, in the hatred of Roderigo.

When breakfast was concluded, Eglantine attended a summons from the baron to see her in the library of the castle.— The Signior received her with a smile of affection, and taking her hand, led her to a seat by his side; she felt encouraged by the tenderness of his manner, to believe that he had repented of his severity; and that the motive of his requesting a private audience, was to express his contrition, and to assure her, he no longer felt inclined to pursue the vengeful purpose he had meditated. The address of the Signior too soon dissipated these pleasing ideas. Eglantine listened to the sophistical arguments, used to divert her from her determination of secrecy, with varied feelings; too unexperienced in the world to be aware of their subtilty, she frequently felt staggered by the artful reasoning of di Rosini; yet her regard for the safety of the being to whom she owed her existence, and subsequent provision and protection, was too indelibly implanted by nature in her mind to be entirely subdued: the sainted Jacquelina had ever taught her to revere the sacred nature of a trust confided to her honour, and these considerations, combined with her native purity of principles, and the benevolence of her heart, determined her to allow no consideration to induce her to swerve from her dictates:—the severity and gloom that had become habitual to the features of the baron, gradually resumed their frowning appearance, as each moment more strongly convinced him of the improbability of his attaining the earnestly desired information, by his endeavours to convict her judgement of error.

"Eglantine! I will no longer condescend to cope with the perverseness of thy nature," said the baron, "convinced of the justice of my demand, and the false heroism of thy refusal, I will no longer seek, by gentle means, to obtain the knowledge I have so vainly requested." Di Rosini for a moment paused; and Eglantine tremblingly awaited the conclusion of his fear inspiring address.

"Is the Signior Roderigo dearer to thee than the Count Adelbert?" resumed the baron. "O! no, my lord; I love no one so well as Adelbert."

"Thinkest thou, Eglantine, thou couldst bear a separation from the Count, with the fortitude thou hast this morning manifested?" enquired the Signior. "A separation!" reiterated his shuddering auditor, "in pity, my lord, suggest not so painful an apprehension."—"Perhaps, Eglantine, there will be found more of reality than apprehension in the suggestion;" returned the baron, perhaps a day may come, and shortly too, when the soft tones of Adelbert's flute shall cease to enliven the dreary solitude of St. Sebastine; when his form shall no longer meet the searching eye of Eglantine, and no hope of re-union shall cheer the hours of absence: then thou mayest rue, too late, the fatal obstinacy of this eventful morn." "My lord, I scarcely comprehend your meaning?" said Eglantine. "Know then," returned the baron, "that the Count Adelbert was entrusted an orphan infant to my care; his sire was my dearest friend, and on his demise, he committed his boy to my charge, with an unlimited authority over his actions and fortune. Should he unite his destiny to a female, independant of my will, his possessions will become mine; and though I have verbally assented to his espousing thee, yet I at any period can retract my promise: and never will I ratify the agreement, till the guilty sire of his promised bride is delivered into my power."

"Impossible!" exclaimed Eglantine, "thou wilt not, thou canst not be so implacable." "Thou wilt find to the contrary," replied the baron sternly, "one word from me, will send thy lover to repel the incursions of his country's enemies; and ere another week shall have elapsed, thou must betray the secret refuge of the Signior Roderigo, or for ever relinquish thy claim on the hand of Adelbert. Attempt not to move me from my fixed resolve," continued the Signior, perceiving the hapless maid about to reply, "my will is unaccustomed to controul, and my determination will remain immoveable, I give thee till to-morrow morning for reflection; weigh well the advantages on either side, ere thou shalt fix on the alternative proposed."

"Stay, my lord," said Eglantine, as the baron motioned to quit the library, "and pardon me, if I refuse the indulgence thou hast just offered; thou hast endeavoured to convince me by reasoning of the error of my conduct; thou, my lord, art well versed in the knowledge of human nature; and conscious of my ignorance of mankind, I felt staggered by thy arguments; but the cruelty of the resolve, with which thou sought to lure me by a selfish motive, to violate the sense of right implanted by the beloved Jacquelina in my bosom, seems to have withdrawn a mist from my eyes, and I feel more than ever impressed with a belief of the rectitude of my perseverance in silence."

The unfolding mind of Eglantine had indeed opened to the selfish and vindictive character of the baron; and though her father boasted but a slight claim on her tenderness, and to part with Adelbert was to part with every thing that gave a pleasure to existence, yet she remembered, that the former had a sacred claim from nature on her reverence and protection;—and even, had no solemn promise enjoined her to silence, Eglantine would have persevered in the fulfilment of what she considered a filial duty, and due to the heaven-born attribute of mercy. Innate virtue had given a firmness to her voice, and a dignity to her mein, as she addressed the baron; whilst the consciousness of undeserved cruelty veiled her mild countenance with an air of haughty superiority, and heightened the pale blush that tinted her cheek into a vermillion glow. "Rash girl! be not too hasty in thy determination," said the baron, "lest thou shouldst repent thy precipitancy.

"No, my lord, I shall never repent sacrificing my happiness, to what I believe to be my duty; but wherefore do I speak of sacrificing my happiness? Shall I not be more blest, though absent from Adelbert, in the consciousness that, to a virtuous principle, I owed the separation, than in reflecting on the enjoyment of his society, if I were to break through a sacred promise, and yield a parent to ignomy and death? and will not my dear, dear Adelbert love me with greater tenderness, when he shall dwell on the motive that induces me to resign him? The baron coloured; he felt unable to reply to the speech of Eglantine, and inwardly supposing that she would continue to supply the bandit with provision, he resolved on secretly watching her movements, believing the greatest probability of discovering the retreat of Roderigo depended on an opportunity of following Eglantine, when she should repair thither with food. In reality, he did not intent to carry his threat of separating the lovers into execution; but the better to give a seeming truth to what he had uttered, and to avoid the remonstrances of Adelbert, he requested he would leave St. Sebastine, giving him a mission to the capital, by which he concealed from the unsuspecting count, that any other motive influenced the request. Adelbert, ever willing to oblige his friend, sought to stifle the regret he felt, on account of leaving Eglantine so depressed in spirits; and had, on the morning in which the Signior di Rosini conversed so seriously with the bandit's daughter, departed from the castle.

The baron, elate with his new plan, repaired in secret every eve to a room, situated next to that occupied by Eglantine; three nights had he watched, when, on the fourth, Eglantine, anxious to impart to her sire the discovery made by the Signior, at an hour past midnight quitted her solitary chamber, and repairing to the place from which she had before taken the viands, filled her basket, and departed on her humane expedition, the baron followed at a distance, his dark dress shaded him from observation, whilst the white garments of Eglantine directed him in the pursuit,—at length she stopped, and stamping three times on the ground, the hidden trap was presently opened, and Eglantine receded from his view. The Signior, concealed behind a wide spreading tree, marked the spot, and as soon as the door was reclosed, he advanced towards it, and cutting a notch in a tree that stood close by its side; he narrowly observed that part of the forest in which it stood; and carefully remarking the road that led from it to the castle, he returned home and retired to his chamber.

Wretched and anxious was the night passed by the bandit; conscious of his own powers of deception, and of the guilty tenor of his conduct, he half doubted the sincerity of Eglantine's professions; and when, on the morn, the sound of the baron and his attendants' approach reached his ears, his doubts almost yielded to conviction;—presently reiterated strokes were heard on the no-longer concealed door; the tortured mind of Roderigo became frenzied with agony, every joint was convulsed, every feature distorted;—he sank upon his knees, he would have prayed, but the full consciousness of the depravity of his past life, rushed with horror on his mind, and choaked the half uttered ejaculations. The door of the cave was violently forced from its hold, and the next moment Roderigo became the prisoner of the injured di Rosini.

"Accursed parricide!" muttered the bandit, as, overcome by the violence of his feelings, he swooned in the arms of two of the domestics, who, regardless o his insensibility, bore him, in compliance with the orders of the Signior, to the dungeons of St. Sebastine. "In this vault," pronounced the baron, unclosing that in which mouldered the form of the blighted Constance, "shall the perfidious Roderigo pass the hours of captivity."

The bandit had revived, ere he reached the castle, but, conscious of his inability to escape from the numerous retinue by which he was guarded, he resolved on persevering in a sullen silence. The attendants by whom he was conducted, led the Signior into the dungeon selected by the baron; and di Rosini, approaching the captive, directed his attention to the tomb—two candles of black wax burnt at either end of the melancholy receptacle.

"Here, till to morrow morn," said the baron, addressing the bandit, "thou shalt be left to reflection!—here, at the tomb of her thy perfidy destroyed, be thy prayers of penitence offered: trifle not with the short period allowed thee, for the coming day will witness the final close of thy fate or mine." "Well do I understand thee," returned the bandit, a smile of gloomy meaning passing over his features; "thy vindictive soul thirsts with insatiate vengeance for my blood; but, baron, thou mayest be disappointed," he muttered in an inward tone, that reached not the ear of di Rosini. The Signior now quitted the dungeon, and securing the door, deposited the key in his pocket, ordering three of his domestics to guard it on the outer side.

Eglantine had listened, with the most apprehensive inquietude, to the noise occasioned by the arrival of the baron and his prey: and ere her grandsire had quitted the presence of his prisoner, she learned from a servant who had been one in the expedition, the cause of the commotion. No sooner had the Signior di Rosini returned to the apartment which he usually occupied during the day, than Eglantine, pale and disordered, rushed into his presence; her hair hung dishevelled on her bosom; and every expression of her mein and countenance bespoke the deepest distress; sinking at his feet, she raised her eyes imploringly on the baron, as in tremulous accents she besought him to have mercy on her devoted sire.—Di Rosini, though obdurate to her entreaties, strove to restore her spirits to composure, and again convince her by arguments of the justice of his proceeding; but Eglantine turned, disgusted, from his efforts, and was deaf to the offered consolation.—Thus passed the dreadful day of Roderigo's captivity. Early in the evening, a message arrived from the bandit earnestly imploring, as a last favour—as a last solace, to be permitted to take a final farewell of his child, ere they parted for ever Eglantine instantly arose, and without awaiting the permission of the Signior, prepared to quit the chamber.

"Be not thus precipitate," said di Rosini, arresting her steps, "ere I consent to the indulgence he requires, I must know whether he deserves my lenity: thinkest thou Antonio that he feels repentant, and resigned to meet a fate he is conscious of deserving?" "He does, my lord," returned Antonio; "he appears, from what we hear him utter, sensible of the errors of his past conduct, and full of tenderness for the lady Eglantine! and he entreated to behold her, in a manner so humble and so urgent, that, unable to refuse, I have repaired to thy presence to submit his wishes to thy pleasure."

The baron acquiesced; and Eglantine, supported on the arm of Antonio, repaired to the scene of her sire's imprisonment. Roderigo met her at the entrance of the vault, and bowing, in apparent gratitude to the man who had accompanied his daughter, he led her to the only seat the cave contained. Re-approaching the door, he forced a rusty bolt on the inner side, that had escaped observation, into its hold; then in silence again advanced towards Eglantine.

"To morrow," said the bandit, bending on Eglantine a penetrating gaze, "di Rosini and myself are to try our skill in single combat; if I fall, he will still exist to glory in the life he has destroyed; but should he be the sacrifice, I shall be delivered into the custody of the fiends who torture without mercy, and smile at the agony they inflict. Such is the baron's decree!" pursued Roderigo, with a demoniac expression; "and such is the fate, to which a dissembling, unnatural child would subjugate a deceived a persecuted parent!"

"Father! what dreadful meaning wouldst thou insinuate?" demanded the shuddering Eglantine. "Heighten not thy criminality," pursued the bandit, in a low, but angry tone; for he wished not the converse to be heard; "seek not by a persistance in falsehood to palliate thy guilt and impose on my credulity: fool that I was! to trust my fate to the disposal of a wretch so incapable of mercy.—What though guilt has marked the course of my existence, since the days of infancy, was it for thee! under the sacred semblance of truth, to bring me to punishment?"

Eglantine, terrified by the ill repressed violence of the bandit, and shoked and surprised at what he uttered felt scarcely capable of articulation; her frame became convulsively agitated, her blood flowed coldly through her veins, and her senses seemed receding as though incapable of supporting the shock. The Signior Roderigo, unacquainted with the refinement of a pure and guileless mind, read in the emotion of Eglantine, a fresh and incontrovertable proof of what he had before felt no doubt in believing; a heavy gloom sat upon his knitting brow, his sallow features became livid. and his dark eyes, beaming with an expression of malignity, were rivetted in firmer attention on the features of Eglantine. "Baron di Rosini, thy revenge shall be disappointed!" he exclaimed, as he drew a small dagger from his bosom; "pleased with the anticipation of thy bloody purpose, thou, with impatient expectation, awaitest the coming morn; but long, long before that period," he continued, with a convulsive laugh, "thy desired victim will be freed from thy detested power."

Eglantine alarmed at the wildness of the bandit's manner, and the delirious fire that shot from his eyes, was about to repair to the entrance of the cave; but he, perceiving her intent, seized her by the arm, and led her into the centre of the dungeon; incapable of resistance, she submitted passively to the will of her sire. The melancholy light, reflected by the sable candles on the lonely repository of her mother's ashes, and the dark walls of the dungeon, united with the but partially-suspected plan of the bandit, diffused an impressive gloom, that overcame her weakened senses;—objects seemed to swim before her sight, her eyes closed, and she sank senseless on the supporting arm of her father.

"Now then the deed of death shall be accomplished!" ejaculated the bandit. "Eglantine! thou shalt not survive to triumph with di Rosini in the destruction of a parent thou hast betrayed. Roderigo raised the deadly implement; for a moment he paused, and glanced a look of wildness round the dreary dungeon. then again turned to execute his purpose;—the melancholy sighings of the blast through the ancient ruin, sounded like the groans of death upon his ear; and awhile he paused irresolute—the hesitation was but short. "What is the bauble life?" he inwardly pronounced; a wild laugh again burst from his lips. "This irresolution is weak and cowardly! Eglantine will not feel! no, no, she sleeps already and never shall she awake again to gladden the eyes of di Rosini—to scoff and hate the memory of Roderigo.—Now then for a fatal stroke!" Again the dagger was suspended with determined aim by the half maddened Roderigo when the tomb of her he had deserted and betrayed, slowly unclosed, and the pale shade of the injured Constance, with solemn movement, rose from the sacred receptacle! the vital stream seemed still freshly to flow from the self-inflicted wound; slowly she glided from the sepulchre, and approaching the receding bandit, with one hand she pointed to the still senseless Eglantine, and with the other to the glittering steel he had continued to hold. The faltering limbs of Roderigo were incapable of supporting his convulsed frame; and subdued by terror and conscious guilt, he fell prostrate to the ground;—in his fall the murderous weapon deeply pierced his side, and heavy groans of mental and bodily anguish burst from his lips;—the attendants, who were stationed as guards, alarmed at the sound, burst into the dungeon; the spectre had vanished; and Eglantine, without motion, was still lying on the ground, at a short distance from the expiring bandit.

Antonio raised the senseless maid in his arms, and two of the men, supporting the Signior Roderigo to a couch, that had been placed in the cavern, a fourth hastened to acquaint the baron of the catastrophe. Antonio bore the unconscious Eglantine to her chamber, and giving her in charge to a female domestic, returned to the scene of death. The wound had proved fatal, and the trembling spirit of the Signior Roderigo had winged its flight to the awful tribunal of its Creator.

A long and serious illness, resulting from anxiety, fatigue, and terror, confined the suffering Eglantine to her chamber;—the bandit had, in the interim, been interred in the recesses of the forest; and Adelbert returned to the shades of St. Sebastine.—Solaced with the society of him she so tenderly loved, and nursed with the most assiduous care Eglantine at length began to recover from the malignant effects of the fever by which she had been attacked; her restoration to health was rapid; and the delighted baron and Adelbert in a few weeks, beheld, with the liveliest emotion of gratitude and joy, her total renovation.—Di Rosini, conscious that to him might be wholly imputed the cause of her illness, had watched with indiscribable anxiety and remorse the progress of her disorder; secretly determining, should heaven restore her to him, by the utmost indulgence and tenderness, to endeavour to regain the affection he feared the harshness of his conduct had for ever forfeited; but the grateful heart of the sweet maid, ever open to the effusions of kindness, gradually repaid with the affection of a child, the parental treatment of the baron.—The day on which the period of her mourning closed the faithful Adelbert received the hand of his beloved Eglantine; every heart was glad on the joyous occasion; the baron liberally distributed his bounty to his numerous vassals, and universal festivity and delight reigned within the walls of St. Sebastine, and its extensive vicinity.

At the earnest request of di Rosini, the bandit's daughter promised not to quit the castle, during the remaining period of his existence; the infirmities of age had increased on him apace, and two years after the union of Adelbrt and Eglantine, he expired in their arms, leaving to the child of his ever-lamented Constance, his immense property.

The Count and Countess, soon after the death of the baron, quitted St. Sebastine, and settling on the paternal estate of the former, passed the remainder of their days in almost uninterrupted felicity; and when, at length surrounded by a virtuous and happy progeny, they paid the debt of nature, they quitted existence with that tranquil delight which results from the consequences of a well-spent life.

THE END.

THE

LAST OF THE VAMPIRES.

A TALE.

BY SMYTH UPTON, ESQ.

WESTON-SUPER-MARE:
PRINTED BY J. WHEREAT, COLUMBIAN PRESS,

M.DCCC.XLV.

THAT by far the greater portion of this tale has never been re-written, may by some be generously considered as an excuse for many faults. Upon the mercy of such persons it is now thrown; with the assurance, that in it, the hope of affording them amusement has been the sole endeavour of

THE AUTHOR.

March 27, 1845.

THE LAST OF THE VAMPIRES.

EPOCH 1st, 1769.

CHAPTER I.

THE HOSTESS.

It was on a cold November night in the year of grace 1769, that a comfortable family party were assembled round a kitchen fire. The representation of a nag's head, suspended from a pole without the house, indicated the place to be a hostelry, as indeed it was; and the presiding deity thereof, an ancient widow, with the two head domestics of her establishment, composed the party which we have already had occasion to notice.

This lady rejoiced in the euphonious name of Gapper, and she was perhaps one of the most important personages in the village of Frampton. Independent of her ability to make up a rubber, with many little services of a like nature too numerous to mention, she was also, without doubt, the most incorrigible gossip, of all the news-loving old ladies we ever remember to have heard of. But it must not be supposed, that although first spoken of, this lady is our heroine, which she most certainly is not; though many of her propensities may occasionally appear in the course of this history.

Mrs. Gapper and her deputies had been employed for some time, upon the present occasion, in amusing each other and themselves, by relating, as undoubted facts, the most horrible ghostly horrors their weak brains were capable of inventing. Now, not to omit a single circumstance of the events of this memorable evening, it may as well be here confessed that the shivering trio had by this time, and by these means, become in fact by far too nervous to think of separating. In a body they would defy the very witches in whom they so firmly believed; but alone—they were by far in too great a state of excitement to think of encountering the imaginary horrors which their own folly had been conjuring up. And Mrs. Gapper, as, yawning, she rubbed her eyes, was heard to make the following sapient observation, namely—that "she was bothered if she knew how it was, but that notwithstanding the lateness of the hour, she did not feel her usual inclination to retire to rest." And in this opinion she was supported by both John and Sally; such names as Victoria or Albert, for people in their station in life, would at that period have been deemed ridiculous.

The night was indeed so terrific that wiser persons than Mrs. Gapper might have found therein a reasonable excuse for alarm. The rain and snow, as it dashed up in torrents against the windows, and the wind, as it roared, and rushed, and whistled, until the nag's head seemed often in danger of being torn from its elevated position, together with the lateness of the hour, the cold and their own ideas, all combined to fill them with fear. And it is uncertain whether, rather than move, they would not have preferred spending the remainder of the night over what had now become the dying embers of their fire, when an incident occurred, which, as it forms one of the most important events in the evening we have been endeavouring to describe, shall be forthwith recorded.

At this crisis a signal for admittance at the outer door attracted the attention of the whole party. And a single stranger, whose clothes reminded one of a rat, when in a state of semi-drownation, was admitted to enjoy the hospitalities of the Nag's Head. Ghosts, bogles, apparitions, and an entire host of disembodied spirits, vanished in an instant; and, at the time when we now take our leave, for a few minutes, of Mrs. Gapper and her establishment, the ideas of both were engaged in a much more profitable manner; the dame herself being on hospitable thoughts intent, and her friends, with one exception, being bent upon doing that which was polite to that one, who was for his part fully occupied in receiving them. And now, bidding them farewell for a while, we shall introduce to the reader's serious attention, without leaving the village, another inhabitant thereof.

Mr. Alphonso Guttle was a gentleman who appeared to have entered the world for the sole purpose of devouring its productions. An epicure he was not, neither can we consider him as a gourmand; for what were the viands he cared not; but eat he must, and eat he did, until that singular piece of vulgarity, his daughter, often expected he would burst asunder, if another mouthful were added to the enormous store. Other habits he had, equally peculiar, but of these we shall take no notice at present, leaving to time the task of developing them, in their proper place.

This gentleman had resided for some time in the village of Frampton; and having frequently come in contact with Mrs. Gapper, those were not wanting who said an affection had sprung up between them. But this could scarcely have been the case, from the circumstance that the feelings of the gentleman were not of sufficient warmth to find an object of adoration in Mrs. G.; although, had such been the case, she was, without doubt, fully capable of returning his affection; for Mrs. Gapper had long been in search of a person worthy to become her second mate; and observing in Mr. Guttle, to use her own expression, "a well-to-do-body—a widower with few incumbrances," she had long been watching him with a wary eye, fully determined to take every advantage, when the enemy should exhibit signs of giving way. But whether Mr. Guttle suspected the amiable intentions of this female Cœlebs, we know not; but as yet no opportunity had occurred of introducing the subject; but this, though it tried her patience, did not intimidate the dauntless Mrs. G., who, to become Mrs. Guttle, of Guttle Grove, had fully made up her mind.

We now leave the village of Frampton, at present our head quarters, and the inhabitants who adorn it, for the contemplation of a far different scene.

CHAPTER II.

THE SCHLOSS OBERFELS.

In passing from one chapter to another, we may be supposed to have, also, in the mean time, passed over several European nations; for we now find ourselves upon the borders of Bohemia. Our journey hither, however, must have been one of a somewhat miraculous nature; for the scene before us was enacting in the great drama of the world at the precise time as that detailed in the foregoing chapter.

In a large, though rude chamber, lighted by a single lamp, which hung suspended from the roof, sat a young female, over whose beauteous brow about 19 years might, in all probability, have passed. They had not gone by without leaving some slight trace behind them; for melancholy was blended with loveliness in that fair countenance, in a manner which added to its sensibility without detracting from its beauty.

The casket which contained this jewel, rude as it was, seemed to be situated in a castle rather than a cottage; for the appurtenances of the room, though few, were rather of a warlike than a rustic kind. Here and there lay, carelessly cast upon the floor, an iron spear or gauntlet; and ever and anon the wind, as it gained admittance through numerous apertures in the wall, agitated an ancient banner, which, torn though it was, still exhibited signs of armorial bearings having been thereon; and which, doubtless carried foremost in the fray, had often excited the adherents of some proud baron to vengeance and to death. It was indeed a curious scene to witness—youth and beauty, age and solemnity, so singularly mixed together.

Melancholy, indeed, had as yet been the life of Gertrude Flors: she had been long a child of adversity. Left an orphan in early childhood, she had since been dependent for support upon a maternal aunt of hers, whose conduct towards her can only be described as very cruel. We now see her confined in an old chamber, supposed to be haunted by beings not of this world, through the caprice of this unkind relative. But scarcely knowing what it was to sin in wilfulness, and confiding in her own innocence, she cared little, so burdensome had her life become, of where she was placed or what became of her. Her greatest misery perhaps consisted in this, *she had no here-*

after to look forward to; for, with the commonest principles of any religion of any kind, she was entirely unacquainted. From her fifth year, to the time of which we now speak, she had seen no human being, with the exception of her aunt, whose disposition was such, that besides requiring a few menial offices at her hands, she kept her merely for the sake of tormenting her; and cared not to teach her ought but obedience to her commands. And the poor child, with the exception of a few vague ideas of a happy infancy, knew nothing of the world in which she had the misfortune to live.

This aunt, Marie Flors, was, with her niece, almost the sole occupant of the Castle Von Oberfels, and the supreme ruler thereof, in the absence of its lord. Some account of her residence within its walls may not be amiss.

In 1730, Marie Flors undertook to preside over the establishment of the Baron Adolph Von Oberfels. Being a stranger she had, prior to this time, been entirely unaware of the general suspicion with which she now discovered the place was regarded. She was, at this time, about twenty-five years of age, and her character was a very extraordinary one; but the mystery with which ladies' ages are usually enveloped, we must here apologise for disregarding.

Her master seemed scarcely to have attained the same age as herself; and he described to her the duties of her situation in the following words:

"The person who undertakes this office will meet with enormous rewards. Once in ten years I shall visit here to give instructions and pay you for your services. Should you die in the interim, I shall immediately be informed of it. I wish you, therefore, merely to keep the place from ruin and guard as much as possible from intrusion."

Endowed by nature with a singularly fearless disposition, Marie, though she perceived something odd in these conditions, yet accepted them instantly. To most persons the solitude of the place would have driven them away; but, with her, not so; and, regarding the situation as a desirable one, where, do what she might, no disagreeable questions would be asked, she closed directly with her noble employer.

Now it is not our intention to drag the reader, step by step, over the series of years, in which one day exactly resembled another, as they were passed by this solitary female; but merely mention how, when on rising the ensuing day, she found herself alone in the dreary mansion, she began to repent, when it was alas too late, of the step she had taken. How, however, she continued to remain there with an attendant, and saw no human being from day to day, except indeed when a stranger, passing by, stopped to take a sketch of the old domains. But when ten years had at length rolled by, and her mysterious master once more visited his estate, it was with astonishment she observed that he did not appear to be older by a single day than when she last beheld him in that very castle; and, though she dared not mention it, it was a matter of the greatest surprise, which was not lessened when, on his second visit, he still appeared to be as youthful as before.

"Can such things be?" she mentally ejaculated, "and yet it is so." But having now become somewhat attached to the place, she gave up her resolution of leaving, and entered upon another ten years of servitude.

It was about this time that she consented to receive an orphan niece under her care; and it was also about this time, or at least for the first time since our acquaintance with her, that she manifested signs of cruelty in her disposition, by her shameful conduct towards the little Gertrude.

Never regarding her education, she nevertheless was accustomed to inflict upon the child great bodily torture; and, although why she behaved thus we are unaware, still beaten, starved, and scolded though she was, so beautiful did she become, that any other heart than that of a demon must have melted at the sight of her undeserved misery. Such, then, was the state of things, both at home and abroad, on the evening whence we date our tale; and it will become our future duty to connect the circumstances heretofore related. Our retrospect has therefore, like most temporal matters, come to a conclusiou; and future circumstances must be touched upon with more precision.

CHAPTER III.

DOUBLE DANGER.

It was on the afternoon of the following day that a great bustle below stairs attracted the attention of the stranger, whose arrival we have seen; and, on descending, to enquire the cause, an extraordinary scene met his eye: rolling about the room, black in the face, and evidently choaking, was Mr. Guttle; while the manner with which he endured the thumps bestowed on his back, by his hostess, shewed his illness to be unfeigned. Each blow seeming enough to stun an ox. As he entered the room, however, Mrs. Gapper rushed passed him, being in that state of mind that she was not exactly aware of what she was about: and Mr. G., too, seemed nearly distracted, when suddenly seizing the milk-jug, and pouring its contents down his capacious throat, by a violent effort he dislodged the stoppage, but was for some time unable to draw his breath. He had, as was his custom, been drinking tea with his friend when the prediction of his daughter had been thus nearly accomplished, to the intense alarm of Mrs. G.

This lady had a singular propensity of superintending what took place in her establishment, without her friends being aware of her proximity. Now, for the pursuance of this laudable project, she had caused to be constructed a kind of small anti-chamber to most of the rooms in her house; and each of these being strictly private, was just capable of containing her somewhat portly person. And, although she would have disdained, as meanness, the application of her ear to the key-hole, yet she frequently condescended to view from these snuggeries, without any man being the wiser, whatsoever mysteries might be taking place within. It was through the treachery of a servant of hers, who had made the discovery, that this circumstance eventually became known, to the great confusion of Mrs. Gapper, who, strenuously as she denied the charge, was nevertheless (we grieve to relate it) considered guilty by most of her credulous neighbours.

Too nervous to think of trusting herself again in the room with her suffering friend, and at the same time enduring much anxiety on his account, Mrs. Gapper now betook herself to one of her inquisitorial chambers, where, having secured herself, she began to ruminate. This was the first opportunity she had had of scrutinizing the appearance of her stranger guest: and with this she was much struck; for, renowned physiognomist as she undoubtedly was, she read something in his countenance, which, again to make use of an observation of her own, "completely dumfounded her." She observed that he was decidedly foreign; and as to his features, there was much beauty and much care displayed in them, whilst an unearthly expression cast over the whole, rendered his *tout ensemble* very remarkable. Again we transcribe a sentence framed by Mrs. Gapper: "What can there be in that man's face, which makes me tremble whenever I look at him?" But the lady was quite incapable of solving her own query. She here, however, broke the thread of her meditations, for a conversation arose which much interested her.

Mr. Guttle, who during this time appeared to have been asleep, suddenly roused himself, and regarded his companion with an expression of terror in his countenance. "What!" she heard him say, "are the dead raised?" And then, lowering his voice, whilst his eager auditor, in the closet, bent forward her head and opened her ears to the fullest extent, "You here, Baron!" continued the old man, "then where am I?" But how horrified was Mrs. Gapper, at what now took place; for the young man, who did not appear to be more than five and twenty years of age, and who had exhibited signs of much alarm at the speech of his companion, now gradually moved behind him; and, as with a pistol he took a deliberate aim at the old man's head, he said, as if in reply to him, "Now, you are on earth, and now ——," and here a loud report took place, a sound was heard as of a body falling to the earth, and all was still.

Mrs. Gapper dropped down, without sense or motion, in her narrow retreat.

CHAPTER IV.

A SUICIDE.—SCHEMES.

THE most important part of a man's life is the end thereof; and this theory has been shewn us, by experience, to be fully true.

It is a sad picture we are now going to gaze upon: Gertrude Florr is no more; that fair flower, which might have been an ornament to creation, is but senseless clay; all that now remains of her is the inanimate corpse which hangs suspended from yonder beam, and from which the spark of life has fled for ever. And if so be that the inhabitants of another world were thought, by guilty minds, to wander in the room thou wast forced to inhabit, then may thy pure spirit hover in that bloody chamber, a witness to the wretchedness and wickedness of man.

It is indeed too true: having, for some slight act of disobedience, been beaten more than it was in human nature to bear, her spirit gave way,—she could not bear it; and, hanging herself from a beam, her melancholy life was over —she was dead. But ere the first part of this history is brought to a conclusion, a few words concerning our friends at Frampton may not be thought amiss.

Notwithstanding the greatness of his danger, the old man's soul had not yet gone to his account. The ball, which touched no vital part, being extracted from his head by one of those wonderful surgical operations which, although more common in our day, were then considered as almost miraculous, he lived in after years in a state of harmless lunacy; which, while it ruined Mrs. Gapper's matrimonial prospects, seemed scarcely productive of any greater evil. But, ere these things are spoken of, it must be told how Mrs. G., arousing from her state of stupor, came forth from her hiding-place, like a butterfly from its skin; or, as an ill-natured person might render the simile, like a snake having cast its skin; how she alarmed her household; how deep was her indignation to find her guest had taken his departure, forgetting, in his haste, to settle a small account between them, which ran, I believe, to the tune of somewhere about the sum of one pound two shillings and sixpence; how she heightened her loss by having the county scoured for the offender, in vain; how she declared "It was too bad in him to run away before she had time to catch him;" how the stranger was supposed to have been of opinion that "he was acquainted with a trick worth two of that;" and, though last not least, how great was the delight of Mrs. G., when her medical adviser pronounced life to be not entirely extinct in the person of her friend.

Hurried by all these opposing and conflicting circumstances, Mrs. Gapper presented rather a ludicrous appearance; and all the inhabitants of her mansion, as they retired to rest that night, fully agreed with her, that they did not remember ever to have passed a more eventful day.

It was a few months after this that Mr. Guttle, who, though restored to health, had never recovered the right possession of his senses, but who was so harmless as to be permitted his liberty as heretofore, was once more admitted to the tea-table of Mrs. Gapper. It was for the first time since his misfortune that he had been thus indulged; and her purpose, in thus trusting herself alone with one of a class to which she bore a decided aversion, was two-fold; first, should an opportunity occur, she was very eager to gratify her curiosity concerning his former life; and, secondly, a woman of the world though she was, she had not yet given up all hopes of recovering, by his means, her one pound, two shillings and sixpence. For, seeing that the two were acquainted, she hoped to learn from the one, how she might best set a trap for the other.

She had, however, taken the precaution to lay John in ambush in such a manner, that should Mr. Guttle be violent, he might be at hand to protect her from his fury, without his being sufficiently near to become cognizant of their conversation. The insanity of Mr. Guttle had not at all injured his appetite, which was as good as ever; and of this Mrs. Gapper soon became most painfully aware, as she watched plate after plate of bread and butter disappear; and about twice in the course of every three minutes, she remarked to her guest, the great price of flour at that time, occasionally informing him, as well, that butter was fifteen pence a pound. The gentleman, however, continued his tea in a happy ignorance of what his hostess was talking about; and she, on her part, did not stop him, from a sanguine expectation of recovering, by his means, her one pound, two shillings and sixpence.

Now Mrs. Gapper was not stingy; and to loose a little money now and then, at an innocent rubber, she had no objection; but, to be deprived of it against her will, was, as she justly observed, "a scandalous thing, and, should she catch that man, she would be the death of him:" at the same time clenching her fists in the air, in a manner which admitted no doubt of the truth of her assertion. "And now," said the lady, as her guest seemed nearly to have assuaged his appetite, "you must tell me all about your adventures before you came here."

"Certainly," replied he, "I was dressing myself, for half an hour or so, and then —"

"But what I want to learn, sir," interrupted Mrs. Gapper, "was about your history, before I had the pleasure of knowing you."

Contradiction is what few madmen will bear. Merely raising his head, the following words were the only answer Mr. Guttle deigned to make:— "Then, my good woman, you should have said so before." And, throwing himself upon a sofa, the loud gutteral sounds which shortly proceeded from his nasal organs, testified his having fallen into a state of repose.

"Well!" grunted the indignant Mrs. Gapper, as she stalked out of the room with the grace of an aged sow, "things is come to a pretty pass now, however: what next, I should like to know." And she again bewailed the losses she had sustained, consequent upon her great loss of *one pound, two shillings and sixpence.*

END OF THE FIRST EPOCH.

EPOCH II.

1775.

CHAPTER I.

A FUGITIVE AND A CONFERENCE.

It was on a beautiful autumnal evening, in the year 1775, that two foot-travellers, a young man, and one of riper years, slowly descended one of those fine mountains with which the more northern districts of England are so celebrated for abounding. The scene was, in fact, one of extreme grandeur; and one with which the skilled eye of a painter would doubtless have been pleased. The verdure, too, near the spot on which they stood, seemed to be more luxuriant than is often to be thereabouts met with. Twilight was coming on apace; and the gracefully curved hill, upon whose summit they were now resting for a while to contemplate the view, seemed gradually to disappear, until it was seen no longer, in the rippling river which rolled at its foot; and whose waters, faintly glistening, appeared even yet to reflect the glories of the declining sun; in itself an object yet still more magnificent than any we have been endeavouring to describe. The rays of this luminary as, surrounded by gorgeously tinted clouds, which floating around it received their lustre solely from itself, it sunk gently beneath the verge of the horizon, appeared upon the point of setting the world on fire.

But as our travellers, wearied by the fatigues of a hard day's journey, refreshed themselves by gazing forth at these glories of creation, they suddenly perceived another fierce red light spring up in an opposite direction, and, as one declined, the other became more distinctly visible.

It was evident that a building of some consequence was enveloped in flames; and, although it seemed almost an impossibility that any aid which it was in their power to bestow could be of service to an edifice which already bore the appearance of dilapidation, it was nevertheless with a zeal at once as laudable as it was characteristic, that with that intention they set forward towards it.

It was as they were passing through the few rude habitations which we shall dignify with the name of a hamlet, and which was situated near the foot of the hill, that a man ran past them at a pace, which whilst it seemed to indicate both terror and that the runner had some particular object in view, was such as to attract the serious attention of the few and simple rustics who crossed his path.

Amongst those who were most astonished at the singular deportment of this individual, may be mentioned our two friends. His appearance was indeed such as to merit almost universal observation; hat he wore none, and his hair, as it hung dishevelled behind him, imparted a wild look to his person; and, in addition to this, the perspiration, as it streamed from his face, purple with agitation, and dropped from thence upon his uncovered breast, gave rise in the mind to horrible thoughts, which it was difficult for the spectator to repress.

We have endeavoured to give the reader some slight idea of a few particulars; but the *tout ensemble* of this remarkable person was such as to be beyond the power of oratory to describe. He carried in his arms a young child, who, from the momentary glance obtained of it, seemed to be the possessor of much infantine beauty; but ere time had elapsed for another stare, the object of such general attention had gone well nigh beyond their view: yet still, as he jumped from crag to crag, in his ascent of the rugged hill, their eyes were yet fixed upon one point, now appearing somewhat like a small speck, near the summit of a distant mountain, the strange man and his child; and when he had entirely disappeared from view, still, still they looked; but, if in anticipation of a re-appearance of the mysterious object, they gazed in vain.

Suddenly, however, the elder traveller, who was

known among his fellow men by the aristocratical name of Mr. Dibbs, darted forward, and, seizing a paper hitherto unobserved, and which had evidently been dropped by the fugitive, quitted the hamlet with his prize, accompanied by his younger friend, almost before the villagers had recovered sufficiently from their excitement to be conscious of their departure. The paper, the right of Mr. Dibbs to purloin which may, by some, be somewhat doubted, bore a very remarkable superscription. It ran thus:—

> "To be opened in ten days from the date hereof, if not claimed by me, in person, before that time.—September 17."

It required all the energies of the old man to resist the eager importunities of the younger one, that he should examine the document before the period specified.

"No, my son," he replied to the eagerness of his companion, "nor even then shall it be opened by me."

It may, peradventure, be hereafter set forth how fortunate or unfortunate, as the reader shall think fit, it was that Mr. Dibbs arrived at this determination.

A muttered "humph" was the only reply of the disappointed youth. And here, for a time, we leave them.

* * * * *

The last of his race was the Lord de Montford, a man possessed, in a singular degree, of power and vices, in which the ill-gotten former enabled him to indulge. Montford Abbey, the residence of this nobleman, was a building of much antiquity; and it is related of its lord, that when in childhood he was accustomed to pass through an aged gallery, upon the walls of which hung suspended the portraits of the fierce-looking old gentlemen from whom he had the honour to be descended, his features, marked even then with a characteristic sternness, which remained there to his dying day, were observed to relax, as he would exclaim, with a glance at his ancestry, "I will outdo ye all!" and, in cruelty, he did so.

Now, upon the self-same day, though at an earlier hour, as that of which mention has been made in the foregoing part of this chapter, took place, also, another incident, which having a connection with it, will now be recorded.

In a dreary out-house, adjoining Montford Abbey, stand two men: the scene is a fearful one; it is one of those of which the mere recital makes the blood run cold,—a disgrace to humanity, and a testimony to the wickedness of man. The looks of the *dramatis personæ* are no less fearful. Red blood, yet warm, stains their murderous hands, and is seen also in pools upon the floor; the same marks are observable, also, on their clothes.

That tall, dark, fierce man, who paces the vaulty chamber to and fro, and strives to force his unwilling countenance into a smile, in a vain endeavour to think himself happy, is the Lord de Montford. That trembling wretch who kneels with clasped hands upon the floor, is the executor of all the chief villainies of his master—one Isaacs by name, who, moreover, is a Jew: not outwardly, however, for few, in his English manner of speaking, and his Christian garb, would recognise a child of Israel. But so it was; and in his insatiable love of gold, which would often lead him to commit the worst of crimes, was observable a characteristic of his race, to which alone, would it were peculiar.

But, see! as our eyes become more accustomed to the darkness of the place, new horrors become, consequently, more apparent. That motionless form upon the ground, is the body of a man. Observe how noble he looks, even in the bitterness of death; but that is passed with him: and mark how almost celestial his features look, contrasted with those of his inhuman murderers. And now another object merits contemplation: that infant, which although uninjured in itself, is smeared with its father's blood; see how it nestles up to the cold body of its lifeless parent. But the curtain falls, and the *tableau vivant* is no longer visible.

We now see the principal actors seated in his

lordship's private study. But their hands are no longer stained with blood; and the only thing which reminds us of the late tragedy, is the poor little fatherless child, which, rolling upon the floor in the happy unconsciousness of infancy, seems perfectly unaware of the loss it has just sustained.

The baron and his confidant seemed both in deep thought. Perhaps some slight remorse might already be actuating their minds to self-accusation. How that may be we cannot tell; but, in all probability, the fair sun, which streamed in through the casement, did not look down upon two guiltier souls than theirs.

Suddenly, however, as he raised his head, and pointed to the child, Lord Montford exclaimed, in a hollow voice, and prefacing his remark with a loud oath, which, for obvious reasons, will not here be recorded,—

"——, what's the use of doing things by halves? If the child must be put out of the way, why not now?

"Never!" returned the other; "it shall never harm you, neither shall you injure it." And here, after making use of an expression, not remarkable for its elegance, he continued, "and now, squire, it is time you should hear of my intention to retire from office; and if I *should* sometimes trouble you for a hundred or two, for the support of this infant, and as a reward for a few other matters, between ourselves, you know ——"

"But, my good man, you are mad!" interposed his generous patron. "What, if I chose, would prevent a bullet of mine from penetrating your sapient skull? or why should I not intercept your passage from the house, when a word from me would make your egress hence impossible? No, no, my good man! a likely joke, truly!" And, if we take into consideration his day's work, the Baron de Montford looked very facetious indeed.

"Well done, squire!" returned his companion, "and now that you have said your say, perhaps other people may speak. In regard to your numerous questions, I shall vouchsafe but two answers, Firstly, then, my lord, as concerns your redoubtable plan of the bullet, your lordship seems to be sadly unaware, not only that 'two can play at that game,' but that I am acquainted with a 'trick worth two of that.' I might take the liberty of reminding your lordship of one or two other proverbs, such as 'honour among thieves,' &c. &c.; and now, in the second place, I have to inform you, squire, of a little circumstance, with which, I suspect, you have hitherto been unacquainted. You must know, then, that considering my precious life somewhat in jeopardy, in your service, I have been of late taking the advisable precaution of leaving a little parcel in the care of my good landlady, entitled within,

'The Confession of John Isaacs,'

and without,

'To be opened in ten days from the date hereof, if not before claimed by me, in person, before that time. JOHN ISAACS.'

This outside envelope is renewed, and dated afresh, upon every dangerous occasion; and I doubt not the good lady * will comply with the request of this confession, in which all your crimes are fully enumerated. Oh, cunning, deeply-plodding, double-tongued squire! You have educated me in crime, for your own accursed ends; you have made a tool of me; you have persecuted me; and now, were you able to do it with safety to yourself, you would take my life; but —," and here the countenance of the speaker lighted with a demoniac glare, " with all your talents, ye are no match for the time-serving Jew."

" A curse upon your cunning, fellow," returned the peer; and then, as if muttering to himself, " She must be bribed," said he.

" And even that satisfaction, squire," returned the other, " you will be deprived of: as I have rendered what you propose impossible; and even had I not, as I quit this neighbourhood to night, it

* Not Mrs. Gapper.

must be with all haste you execute your notable plan; which would fail again, as I have another copy on my person, like to the first, and which, like it, is entitled ——"

"Peace, babbling fool!" roared the other. "Marian is dead; Evelyn is ——, and now would *you*, a creature of my own forming, as it were, would *you* interrupt me in my course? Never!" and, guided by his lordship's hand, a ball, passing within an inch of his companion's head, had well nigh terminated his mortal career for ever. Instead of this, however, finding his position somewhat uncomfortable, he was preparing to quit the room, when the cries from without informed these two worthies that the abbey was in flames.

Deferring, therefore, his revenge, for a period more seasonable, the Jew, snatching the child from off the floor, took his departure with it through the window, leaving his noble employer to his fate; and, the room being situated upon the ground floor, that circumstance enabled him to escape with greater facility than he might otherwise have done. He was pursued, for a short time, by the servants of Lord Montford; by whom they were instructed to take the fugitive, alive or dead. But, more anxious to save their own property from the flames than to satiate the fury of their lord, these domestics, having chased him across the lawn, returned for that purpose.

The flight; the observation taken thereof; the loss and capture of the important paper, so big with the fate of three individuals; the conflagration, as it appeared at a distance; with other matters, consequent thereupon, we have made mention of heretofore. The Jew, however, had re-possessed himself of his confession, No. 2; and this, in fact, and not the other, was the document he lost in his flight.

CHAPTER II.

THREE TETES A TETE.

It was nine years after this time, when we again resume the thread of our story. In a squalid chamber, in one of the most wretched districts which disgrace the metropolis, sat two children, as singular for their loveliness as was, upon the other hand, their residence, for the meanness of its appurtenances.

Without the house, too, all seemed disconsolate: disagreeability, if there is such a word (there ought to be), appeared to abound. These two little girls, for such they were, seemed also to be depressed by the state of the atmosphere; at all events something weighed upon their minds.

"I wonder, Rose," said one, who looked older than her companion, "for what reason it is that your uncle behaves in so extraordinary a manner?"

"I am sure, Mary, I know not," was the reply. "He has again, you see, left that paper. Here it is:—

'To be opened in ten days, from the date hereof,

if not claimed by me, in person, before that time.'

How very curious," continued she; "and the way in which we live: do you know he never hires a house, nor lives in one of his own; but we lodge for nothing in any old deserted place like this; and sometimes without so much as an hour's notice, he quits it, and hides himself and me in some building of the same sort; but which, if possible, is yet more obscure than the former one. I once thought," she proceeded, "but no, I must not speak of that now: and had you not better leave me, Mary? for he is always more unkind after you have been here; and I expect he will soon be back."

The other complied; and, having kissed her friend, stepped forth into the street.

It was about two hours before, that a man had quitted the dwelling through the same aperture. Isaacs, for it was he, was somewhat changed in appearance since we last heard of him; looking rather ninety than nine years older since that time; he had also become more sullen and morose.

It was after many turnings and windings, that, after perambulating first dirty lanes and alleys, and afterwards streets, gradually of a more and more respectable grade, the Jew finally rested before a splendid mansion in the extreme western end of London. Here, having gained admittance, he was hushered through vast halls and heaps of gorgeously attired menials, until he stood, once more, in the presence of the Lord de Montford. The few passed years had left but little trace behind them upon the countenance of his lordship: the same grim expression sat there still. It was some time since he had seen his accomplice, upon whom time had made a much greater impression than on himself. "You here again! what is your will?" said he to the Jew, whose characteristic reply ran as follows.

"Come to trouble your lordship for a little money!—two hundred pounds."

"It is yours," said his lordship; "and now, my good man, what has become of the child? I forget its sex;"—and he paused for a reply.

"A—a—boy, my lord."

"Indeed!" said the other, "I had always been under the impression of its being a female. At all events, however, it must instantly be put out of the way; for which purpose I will make the two hundred four."

"Once for all, my lord, the child is of use to me, and shall live. Get the confession; murder the child, as you did its father before it; and then you might e'en murder me too: *but* not to-day, my lord."

"Well, then," said the other, "to change the conversation, whereabouts is your town residence, Mr. Isaacs?"

"Oh, would you not like to know it, squire! but it is a question I must decline to answer. How pleasant would it not be, to take a stroll towards it, some fine evening, and, having cut my throat, stolen the child, and burnt the paper, to sit down entirely at ease, and fancy yourself secure."

His lordship, who by no means enjoyed this kind of banter, was again very coolly preparing a conclusion to the life of his friend.

"The confession! squire," sneered the Jew, as, possessing himself of the money, he slunk away.

Thus ended a second conference between these two worthies.

A servant who entered the room soon after, brought the news of a visitor waiting for admission below.

"Shew him up," said the peer; "and remember that the man who has just left me, is on no account to be again admitted."

"The Baron Von Oberfels," announced the servant; and that dignitary entered the room. The young German, however, for such he was, appeared to be a stranger; for, slightly starting, and with an assumption of surprise, he exclaimed,—

"It is Evelyn Lord de Montford, I have the honour to wait upon."

To which the other very courteously replied, and with an affectation of tears,—

"Any friend of my late lamented brother is welcome here."

And, after this singular introduction, a great intimacy was established between them, ere the conclusion of the visit.

Evelyn de Montford and Von Oberfels had been friends upon the continent; and, upon the arrival of the latter in England, his first visit was to the house of his friend, whom he was doubtless shocked to find no more.

To an enquiry from the other, respecting his residence in town, he replied, "Why, to tell you the truth, my means keep me in the more vulgar districts. I reside in a house somewhat unfrequented; inhabited, indeed, solely by an old man and a girl, who appear to me to be a very mysterious pair: by the bye, I passed the former not far from your door.

"His name?" shouted de Montfort.

"I believe him to be called Isaacs."

"'Tis he, by heaven!" roared the other; and, as if wild, he performed some very surprising evolutions. "Excuse me," he continued, observing his companion to stare at these singular demonstrations of joy; "but that man has ever been the bane of my existence, and, could you but conduct me to him, that I might —— might take him into custody—and claim for ever my gratitude, demand any service at my hands, it is yours."

"And he is yours," said Von Oberfels; "but no violence must be used; upon which condition I am ready to guide you to his dwelling to-night."

Having fixed the plan for their evening's entertainment, the new friends separated.

"Isaacs!" shouted de Montford, as he was once more alone, and with a howl of exultation, "you are mine yet—mine, mine, body and soul,—you mine, mine, for ever!"

CHAPTER III.

A CHANGE OF RESIDENCE; AND A DISAPPOINTMENT; WITH OTHER MATTERS.

Some circumstance or other seemed to have made the Jew suspicious. No sooner had he returned, than he desired his charge to prepare for an instant removal from their temporary home. Their small preparations being soon completed, hand in hand they quitted the miserable abode, for one which, if it were possible, was still more comfortless. The day, which has been already described as a disagreeable one, had cleared up as it proceeded, and now the rain had entirely ceased to fall.

Their way fell over old London bridge, and they stopped for an instant to gaze from the balustrade of that venerable pile, at the busy waters beneath.

Afternoon was just verging into twilight, but the hazy state of the atmosphere prevented any of the celestial bodies from being visible. The peculiarity of her situation was a topic frequently uppermost in the mind of Rose; and during this walk she indulged as usual in her melancholy retrospections. Her uncle, if he were such, treated her with rigour, if not absolute unkindness; yet, whither should she flee for protection? Alone, in the wide world; beset, too, with dangers and enemies she knew not of, she had but one friend; that friend, however, was one of the scarcest of the class—she was a true one.

This was the young person Mary, a conversation between whom and Rose will be found in the commencement of the last chapter. This Mary had been the servant of a Mrs. Dibbs, a singular old lady, who, firmly believing herself a lineal descendant of King Henry the Eighth, and rightful sovereign of the English realms, had disinherited her only child, for marrying a respectable woman of his own rank in life. This old lady, though known to be rich, departed this life suddenly one fine morning, leaving behind her neither will nor money: that is to say, no such articles could be discovered. Indeed, even her funeral expenses had been defrayed by the parish, to the vast indignation of several red-faced churchwardens.

Her services being, therefore, no longer required, Mary now returned to the residence of her mamma; and it was soon after this important domestic event, that she became acquainted with the mysterious Rose, whose singular history excited her interest.

Mentioning, accidentally, the now deserted mansion of her late mistress, the Jew secretly determined to examine it himself, and that if the result was satisfactory, he would occupy it with his charge, when a change of residence should become desirable. This was the house, then, to which the two were now proceeding, and to which, for a while, we must continue to follow them. Rose was aroused from the train of thought into which she had fallen, by a melancholy strain, which harmonized well with her disposition; and, on looking round, she observed a wandering Savoyard, who, far away from his mountain home, was thus endeavouring to obtain subsistence. This person imploring alms, she replied, with tears in her eyes, "Alas! my poor man, I have nothing to bestow."

The event was but trifling; nay, perhaps in itself insignificant; but the thought that some might perhaps be equally, or even more, unfortunate than herself, served to compose her mind; and a silent prayer ascended to heaven, that if she had ever riches, she might use them well.

It was not long after this, that after turning down a narrow alley, for it was no better, she was installed into her new home. That night the two barons repaired to the house of the Jew. No friendly welcome, however, greeted their unheeded entrance through the desolate portal: they left no room unscoured, but in vain; all he had hoped to secure had fled. At the very moment, in fact, when every obstruction to what he fancied felicity, seemed absolutely within his grasp, all is suddenly snatched from him, to the destruction of his fondest hopes. Again would he have to toil, lay plans, and bribe spies; perhaps, too, to meet again with a like result; so discouraging is failure.

But another person, seeming on the same errand as themselves, encountered them ere they departed: this was the before-mentioned Mary, who, however, half suspecting their new residence, was not so concerned as she might have been, at this sudden disappearance of her friend. This she was at one time just on the point of intimating to the two strangers; but suspecting their sinister looks to be fraught with ill to Rose, she remained silent on a subject of which she little suspected the importance. Venting their rage in impotent words, the strangers departed; and, after a renewed and fruitless search, she followed their example.

It was a matter of some astonishment to the Israelite, to find the confession, dropped by him on the evening of the fire, lying upon the table of his new residence; and, in a short time, Mr. Dibbs himself entered the room, who instantly recollected Mr. Isaacs; though, by the bye, Mr. Isaacs had not the slightest idea of ever having seen Mr. Dibbs before. That gentleman, however, introduced himself; promising to return the unopened document of the other, if he was able to discover for him the hidden will of the late Mrs. Dibbs; which paper, after a long search, was at length found sewn up in a night-cap, formerly in the possession of that lady.

It was not many days after this event, that an old woman, accompanied by a younger one, demanded admission to the Baron de Montford. As the visitors of this peer were often very singular-looking people, instead of meeting with the reception they might have anticipated, they were readily admitted. The elder of these ladies deserves a description: a huge straw bonnet, drawn over a flaxen wig of similar dimensions, formed her head-dress; whilst a green flannel wrapper composed the nether garment of this singular female. She also appeared to be suffering from lame feet; and such a constant snorting, sneezing, sniffing, coughing, and even spitting, did she keep up, that it was difficult for a spectator to refrain from laughing at her misfortunes.

The servant who announced her, seemed to have much curiosity concerning her business with his master; and it was not until he had thrice been desired to do so, that he left the room. The old lady continued her grimaces 'till the door was closed, when, throwing off her green flannels, her straw-bonnet, and her wig, she disclosed as their contents, the form of Mr. Isaacs, the Jew.

"He-he-he!" chuckled the unwelcome intruder; "very well, indeed! so I'm not to be admitted, eh? Oh, my dear friend, it would require a wiser head than yours to keep me out. And now," continued he, "permit me to present to you the Lady Rose de Montford, and your most respectable niece;" and then, addressing her, he resumed: "This, my dear, is your uncle; who is about to restore you to the estates of your father, whose throat he cut for what he is now tired of. But, my thousand pounds first, you know; and then, my dear squire, I leave you in quiet possession of your affectionate niece."

"I can obtain her without," replied his lordship, and he levelled a pistol at his head. This time his aim was more successful; but the shot was returned: and thus expired the unfortunate, but not naturally wicked, executor of the crimes of another.

Lord Montford did not, however, expire, like his victim, without a groan; he rose from the floor, to which he had fallen, and, clapping his hand to his breast, gasped out the single word—"Water!"

His servants conveyed him to his own chamber. But we will close his history before proceeding.

It was three hours before a word escaped his lips: he had lain until that time as if in a trance, when he called for his niece, who had been brought instantly to his bed side; but, ere her arrival, nature had again given way. Horribly his eyes rolled round in their sockets, in the excess of his agony. "Off! off!" he cried, pointing to a creation of his brain at the foot of his bed. "Off! off!" he exclaimed again; and terror overcoming, as it were, nature, he endeavoured to leap up, with a desperate effort—a final effort. But the exertion was too much for his sinking frame; his glaring eyes, darting almost from their sockets, suddenly became dim; his death-shriek, loud and shrill, rent the air; this was succeeded by a silence yet more terrible—all was still. *Stulte! hac nocte repetunt animam tuam; et quæ parasti cujus erunt?*

The lights burnt dim, as the domestics, regarding each other with silent horror, stood as if spellbound to the spot. The little Rose dropped down upon her knees; the dying shriek of the departed seemed yet to ring in her ears. Again she heard the last invocation "Off! off!" Again she saw his last gestures. In short, the break of day found her yet upon her knees, beside the body of the dead. A paper discovered on the person of the Jew, in fact the celebrated confession upon which he prided himself so much, after narrating several crimes of a minor kind, related how the writer, upon a certain day there specified, had murdered Lord de Montford, immediately upon his return from the continent, at the instigation of his brother; how the child brought up by him, was the sole and lawful issue of the deceased nobleman; and, after proceeding in such a strain, the document concludes in the following remarkable manner:—

"And now, be ye whosoever ye may, and under what circumstances whatsoever, who shall peruse this document, seize, arrest, or cause to be arrested, that double-dyed traitor, the Lord de Montford. I denounce him as a murderer, a perjurer, a robber; nay, did I but lay to his charge one half the sins I could impute to him, his whole nation would rise with one accord, to condemn a malefactor so base. And now, for confirmation of what I have alleged, search the out-houses adjoining Montford Abbey; you will there have more than proof of all that I have said; and I beseech you as men, as Christians, nay, as creatures possessing the attributes of humanity of one more deeply injured than his very brother."

Mr Dibbs died soon after this time; but his widow will be found an important person, in the third part of this history.

On the fate of Mary, history is silent.

It is supposed that the Lady Rose de Montford has also departed this life: she never married, and it has been considered the manner in which she had been brought up, was productive of much injury to her constitution. It has also been concluded that the bones of her father received a decent interment; for, although the matter was conducted with privacy, and the villagers are not communicative on the point, a plain white marble flag, in the private chapel of Montford Abbey, seems to bear out the supposition. Upon this flag are merely inscribed the words,

"Evelyn de Montford."

END OF THE SECOND EPOCH.

EPOCH III.

1780.

CHAPTER I.

THE PARTNERS.

TEN years have passed away. The old earth still continues in being; but many of her inhabitants who then, in the midst of youth and happiness, thought all the world was made for their enjoyment, are returned to that dust from which all came, and to which everything must assuredly return. The village of Frampton still retains its original appearance; and although many of its occupants have, during the ten years passed, been gathered to their fathers, yet it is with much de-delight that we have to inform the reader that neither of our old acquaintances were amongst this number.

Mrs. Gapper still held sway over the Nag's Head; but not alone, for she had taken into partnership a certain Mrs. Dibbs, of whom a waggish neighbour once justly remarked, that she was "a werry eccentric animal."

Mr. Guttle, too, was still the lord of Guttle Grove. But he had, just at the commencement of this second part of our history, experienced a very sad affliction: this was the death of his only child; who, though she has been mentioned once, cannot be considered as one of our *dramatis personæ*.

This was a very heavy sorrow to the poor old man, who seemed to be quite borne down with grief. We, upon one occasion, touched upon the vulgarity of the departed; but this mattered not to him—he knew it not; if she was vulgar, he was not genteel; but this he knew, that she was his daughter, his only relative, his devoted servant, his only friend; and now she was gone: never more, in this world, should he again behold those eyes, which, for many a long and weary day, were the only ones which had beamed with affection upon him.

"Oh! that it had been me," he cried, as he pressed his hands upon his burning temples; "I am old, and would not have been missed. And shall I never see her again? Am I deprived for ever of my only child? Oh, that I could follow her!" And, as he flung himself upon the body, in such agony of mind as a father lamenting for his child can only know, he truly longed to die.

It was about this time that the old man was never observed to ramble as formerly; and in a short time it became obvious, to the great delight of his friends, that he had at last recovered the possession of his proper senses. It is supposed that the intensity of his sorrow had set in action some dormant properties of the brain; and, however this might have been, it is certain that reason was now returned.

No one rejoiced with more sincerity at this happy change than Mrs. Gapper, who soliloquised within herself, that "It was rather late in the day, to be sure; but better late that never, and there was no knowing what *might* happen." Whether or no she counted her chickens before the period of their incubation, remains to be proved.

It has already been mentioned that Mrs. Gapper had taken into partnership a certain Mrs. Dibbs; how she came to do a thing so very extraordinary for her, I cannot say, but so it was. This Mrs. Dibbs had a habit of making collections for the poor; and several people who had supplied her with money for this purpose, very justly suspected that it went towards the private expenses of this humane lady. At this time, however, these worthies had not lived together above a month, and had yet to begin their first quarrel; but it could scarcely be supposed that two such opposite characters could continue long in amity, Mrs. Dibbs being extremely serious, and partial to psalms singing, whilst Mrs. Gapper's peculiarities have already been represented.

Mrs. Dibbs was bringing up, out of pure charity,

she informed her friends, a young female, about whom there seemed to be some little mystery; for whilst her guardian acknowledged her to be no relation, she brought her up with too much care for her kindness to be proceeding from purely disinterested motives. This young person, who was usually known as Charlotte Dibbs, although hints had escaped the old lady that she was entitled to another name, was considered, by Mrs. G. and Mrs. D., to be one of the best and prettiest young females in the village; and that they did so is the more surprising, from the girl being a complete amazon, and so extremely full of mischief, that it is with much pain we shall have to record several very unlady-like tricks which she played off upon the old girl, her guardian, for it was by this epithet she usually styled Mrs. D.

It was very probable that this lady borrowed her idea of collecting money for the poor, from some book, for she had an extraordinary habit of copying the manner of any heroine with whose history she had been interested. It is related of her having, upon one occasion, nearly starved herself to death, whilst imitating the conduct of an unfortunate nun.

Let not any one suppose, for an instant, that Mrs. G. had ceased to grieve over the memory of her one pound, two shillings and sixpence; on the contrary, the recollection of that sad mishap was still, at intervals, accustomed to sour her temper, and turn her strong bohea into something worse than gall. But, perhaps, one of the best parts of the affair was, that she had, for some length of time, been adding to the account the extravagant interest of one penny per week. Her expectation of regaining this is supposed to have been very faint.

Another circumstance has yet to be recorded. The hostesses were about to give a rural *fête*, at which about fifty neighbours would be entertained. This muster was too strong for Frampton; but several other villages would supply guests for the great occasion. These were to be divided into two parts: one, having Mrs. Gapper for its head, would spend the evening in cards, and other *rational* amusements, at the conclusion of an elegant supper; while a second, under the dominion of Mrs. Dibbs, would pass their time in a far more profitable manner: a plain tea being finished, the remainder of the night would be devoted to a serious lecture, read by the silvery voice of Mrs. Dibbs herself; and, to vary the entertainment, it was understood that a certain well-known and eloquent gentleman, a Mr. Huggins, or Parson Huggins, for by both of these names he was known, would recite some poetry of his own composition.

This *fête* would not, however, take place for a

few weeks; by which time Mrs. Gapper hoped she should be able to wheedle Mr. Guttle to honour the assembly with his august presence. The following specimens may be interesting:—

A card of invitation from Mrs. Gapper to the friends of that lady:—

Mrs. Gapper presents her compliments to ———, and requests the honour of their attendance at an evening party at her house, on Thursday, 28th inst.

A card of invitation from Mrs. Dibbs to the friends of that lady:—

Dear Friend,—

Your presence is particularly requested, on the 28th instant, for the contemplation of a lecture, entitled "Cream for the Good; throw Skim-milk at the Wicked." Your friend and sister,

DOROTHY DIBBS.

N.B. Mr. Huggins will be present.

CHAPTER II.

A FEAST AND A FRAY.

THE day has arrived; the preparations are concluded; and when the company assemble, all things will be found ready for their reception.

The entertainers were looking forward to the scene of their hospitalities with three very different sources from which they intended to derive amusement, which, in the opinion of the sapient Mrs. Dibbs, is ever blended with instruction. Mrs. Gapper, however, on the other hand, considered that the absence of instruction constituted enjoyment, and said so; whereat Mrs. Dibbs was extremely shocked, and spreading her hands *ad sidera,* somewhat in the attitude of the gentleman mentioned by Virgil, she could only utter "Alas!" as she thought of the depravity of the world in which she lived. She was looking forward to the feast with the hope of collecting vast sums of money, which well she knew the poor souls for whom it was given would never see.

Her partner, meanwhile, who though she was

sometimes wicked enough to be merry, was nevertheless far nearer to perfection than her friend, who though she professed more, it is much to be feared had more need of reformation, was delighted with the prospect of hearing, at last, the eventful history of the mysterious Mr. Guttle, from his own lips. We refer those who would think Mrs. Gapper inconsistent, in submitting to so expensive an amusement, to an observation which occurs towards the end of the first epoch of our history. In the third place, Miss Charlotte was looking forward to the party with much joy, on account of her having made a determination to play off some famous tricks upon so excellent an opportunity.

The first person who arrived was an aristocratic, though ancient, matron, of the name of Fitzpeagreen, and she was the bosom friend, and sister-gossip, of Mrs. Gapper. The room dedicated upon this occasion to the reception of the numerous visitors, was a peculiarly large one, for so comparatively small a house as that in which it was situate; and as it was frequently made use of by clubs, who there transacted business of the most private and important nature, it was of course not destitute of an invisible chamber, from whence Mrs. Gapper could become aware of whatever was going on; indeed, this lady had formed a notable plan of congregating there some society of Freemasons, whose mystic signs she would, for a due consideration, brand forth to the public; perhaps, good soul, forgetting, in her haste, that new mysteries would immediately be instituted. But this is not to the point: the room was mentioned to inform the reader of the manner in which it was laid out, one part being dedicated to the secular, the other to the spiritual members of the festivity; and, in order to divide it the more effectually, a low rail was put as a partitition, which, however, was not above three feet high; and, as party-spirit was anticipated to run high during the day, the hostesses had happily agreed that this should not be the cause of any wrangling between them. But Mrs. Gapper nearly offended her partner by the look of superiority she gave when Mrs. Fitz-peagreen, in all the pride of a brown silk gown slashed with blue, could impart, entered into her partition, while that of Mrs. Dibbs was yet without a guest.

The room began to fill. The next arrival was that of the two Misses Bolster, good-humoured, fat, vulgar girls, who cared not to conceal their rusticity, calling out "Lawk!" and expressing their admiration of whatever surpassed in its kind that which they possessed at home. A great commotion on the other side the partition now attracted universal attention thither; it was caused by nothing less than the arrival of the Rev.

Ptolemy Huggins, whose reception was such as became a person of his exalted station, talents, character and rank: "Mr. Huggins, sir, we're proud to see you," said Mrs. Dibbs; and a clapping of hands ensued, during which the reverend gentleman bowed repeatedly, a white kid glove and its contents being laid upon that part where his heart, if he had one, ought properly to have been. Amongst the more distinguished of Mrs. Dibbs' guests, was Mr. Muddle, an ancient hypocrite, and a Miss Figginbottom, a speculating spinster, attired in a pale blue, that suited admirably her sixty years. Besides these, Charlotte Dibbs was of course with her aunt.

The two tables were spread as follows:—

TABLE OF MRS. G.

Sel	Cold Turkey	Salt
Pommes de terre sans leur habits	Punch	Pommes de terre avec leur habits
	Ham	
Tarts	Epergne	Tarts
Roast Pigeon		Roast Rabbit
	Ham	
Cold Pie	Punch	Cold Tongue
Sel	Cold Round of Beef	Sel.

TABLE OF MRS. D.

Weak infusion of Tea

Row of Empty Plates

Bread with Butter

Bread without Butter

Sugar

Milk

Bread without Butter

Bread with Butter

Row of Empty Plates

Weak infusion of Tea

One young lady imprudently remarked something about wolves in sheeps' clothing, which the guilty mind of Mr. Huggins construed into a challenge to his table, and administered a severe rejoinder; but the *mens conscia recti* of Mrs. Dibbs prevented a warm dispute, for she knew their conduct to be without reproach.

Miss Bolster enquired of another young lady if she had yet perused that delightful romance, called "Aldiborontiphoskiforniosticos; or the seventeen-bladed clasp-knife of the haunted hut." To which question the other young lady replied, "Oh, dear no, she certainly had not:" but, at the same time, looking very much as if she had.

Such light conversation as this, however, was not going to pass unheeded by the other table; and it was with uplifted hands and eyes that Mr. Huggins exclaimed, "Oh! poor foolish moths, how long think ye to hover round the candle unscathed? While ye, like the poor wretched flies, waste your time in unprofitable nonsense, behold how we, the representatives of the industrious ants and bees, make hay while the sun shines, and lay up stores against an evil and an adverse day."

Many observations were here made at once; one being heard to remark his past ignorance that bees made hay; another, mentioning the case of the fox and the grapes, was heard to marvel if Mr. Huggins would not, if permitted, be delighted to join their partition himself; and, at the same time, Mrs. Dibbs being heard to inform her visitors of how the reverend gentleman's speech had called to her recollection an invariable practice of hers, of endeavouring to collect money for the support of her poorer fellow-men, and who, though in less affluent circumstances than herself, she could never cease to remember were her brethren the same.

Here Miss Charlotte most unfortunately put in, "If you recollect, ma'am, the gown you have on was paid for by the last subscription."

"Base, unnatural ingrate," said Mrs. Dibbs, as she struck her fists upon the table, and really looked very furious indeed, "is it for this that I have nursed you, and fed you, and clothed you, and slaved for you, like a—like a—I don't know what?—"

Miss Charlotte, it seems, had no mind to be hauled over the coals in this manner; she merely, therefore, observed, "Aunt, do you remember what I saw, last Friday six weeks?" and the words appeared to possess a talismanic influence: nothing more was said.

The meal had now, upon both sides, come to a conclusion: the major part of the one portion of the company were nearly fuddled with the quantities of punch which they had swallowed; but the extreme weakness of the tea had made the opposition more sharp and ostentatious than ever. Now it was that Mrs. Dibbs began to deliver the lecture which, composed by herself and Mr. Huggins, bore the imposing title of—" Cream for the Good; throw skim milk at the Wicked."

Not another word had escaped the orator's lips, when the stern Miss Figginbottom, mistaking the real meaning of the words, comprehending not the hidden meaning, but misunderstanding, that it was not in reality the wrong doers who were thus to be actually drenched; and being, moreover, actuated by a desire of shewing off her zeal before Mr. Huggins, suddenly rose from her seat, and seizing a large milk-jug, which had not, unfortunately, been taken away, ejected the whole of its contents towards the opposite end of the room, and the disagreeable shower lighted upon the head of a hapless spinster, who was employed, at the moment, in slipping a pair of loaded dice into a cavity in her sleeve. By no means expecting this untoward event, the aged damsel was extremely indignant thereat; and, leaping over the boundary, she proceeded to the unlady-like expedient of pulling the cap of her adversary from off her head; and her delight, when the flowing ringlets of the latter came off at the same time, may be conceived better than described. A demoniac grin imparted to her features, already begrimed with milk, a look so absolutely diabolical, that even Mr. Huggins retired slightly from her path.

The victorious lady, as she took her departure at an earlier hour than she had previously anticipated, was followed by cheers and groans from the different sides of the room.

Sometime after this sad affair, as Mrs. Dibbs was getting more and more enthusiastic as she proceeded in her discourse, she was observed to turn very pale, and remarked in a feeble voice, that somehow or other she really felt very unwell indeed; and, in a few seconds, several others made a like discovery: they, too, felt very unwell; so much so, indeed, that excess of pain, caused them to run about the room, howling, groaning, rubbing their unthink-of-ables, and, in fact, altogether conducting themselves in a very remarkable manner. The Rev. Ptolemy Huggins, too, was not exempt from the general attack; and, as the agony of his inner man forced him alternately to skip, scream, jump, bellow, and perform many other surprising evolutions, he really presented a very extraordinary appearance. His feelings were truly such that he, we hope for the first time in his existence, though there may be doubts upon the subject, uttered a word, which can only be recorded as having commenced with the fourth, and concluded with the fourteenth letter of the English alphabet. And a better proof of the reality of this sudden illness can scarcely be given, than that this circumstance, which, at any other time would have expelled the offender from the gifted congregation, passed unheeded by the afflicted assemblage.

"Oh!" exclaimed an old lady, who was chiefly remarkable from a crimson turban, which gave an expression of much ferocity to her features, "to think of my living to die like this! Pisoned, pison in the tea, O-o-o-o-o-o-o," continued she, as a sharp pang, shooting through her inwards, interrupted her lamentations, by nearly extending her upon the floor. The supposition of having imbibed poison, now filled them with more alarm than before; and one and all declaring they would not live to die in a beer-house, trotted off, as well as they could, to their own residences; concluding, in this eccentric manner, the festive entertainment of Mrs. Dibbs. Mrs. Gapper's, however, had gone off in a much more satisfactory way; for, with the exception of several individuals making the discovery that they had been sitting upon some eggs, thereby imparting a singular look to that part of their dresses injured by the inelegant contact, one and all had declared themselves much gratified; and though they had not been honoured with the company of any such distinguished person as the Rev. Ptolemy Huggins, yet, from the opportunity they had now had, of gaining an insight into the disposition of their more serious neighbours, an opinion was prevalent that more was said than done among that respectable corps.

CHAPTER III.

LEARMONT CASTLE.—MISS FIGGINBOTTOM.

Mrs. Gapper had at length been gratified in her earnest wish of hearing the past history, which seemed so fraught with mystery, of her friend Mr. Guttle. As it happens to form a connecting link to several circumstances which may have appeared singular, it shall be laid before the reader; not, however, in the exact form in which it was delivered by Mr. G. which was interspersed with many superfluous remarks, but in one in which, without speaking himself, he will be spoken of.

The father of the individual in question had been for many years the head domestic of Learmont Castle, the seat of Sir James Learmont, who being a Baronet, was, moreover, a Knight of the Bath and M.P. This gentleman had a great regard for his old servant; and when his son was old enough, he entered the castle as my lady's page, being afterwards promoted to the office of footman. Sir James Learmont, though without a male heir, had two daughters; and few there were, among the numerous visitors at the castle, who was not striving to obtain them in marriage, either for themselves or some relation.

Amongst these was a certain young German, the Baron Von Oberfels, who had long been understood to be the accepted suitor of the eldest; indeed, the younger one, Constance Learmont, was as yet scarcely of an age to think of matrimony.

The reader shall here become acquainted with what Mr. Guttle, himself, was unaware. This young nobleman was one of that horrible class, the Vampires! He had sold his soul to the evil one, for the enjoyment of perpetual youth; being bound, besides, to what are understood to be the penalties of that wretched and accursed race. Every tenth year a young female was sacrificed to his infernal master. Mary Learmont was to be the next victim; may she escape the threatened doom. But the hour is come: as a lamb to the sacrifice she is led to the altar: she is a wife; what will she be?

The baron and his bride departed on his wedding tour. Her father and mother never hear of her more. Like Israel of old, being bereaved of their children, they were bereaved; and the malediction of another father was added to that account to which the Last of the Vampires would have to answer. The frequency and enormity of his manifold offences had rendered callous the heart of this wretched man.

Time rolled on; and, his aged master being dead, Mr. Guttle had settled in Frampton, to spend in independence the rest of his days: he could tell Mrs. Gapper no more. How a sudden and unexpected interview had taken place, between the baron and himself, and the consequences thereof, she knew already.

Constance Learmont had made a happier marriage than her sister. A young captain in the army, of the name of Hastings, was her choice. She, however, had died in giving birth to a daughter, her second, having had another daughter some years before.

It was with mingled astonishment and awe that Mrs. Gapper gave credence to this remarkable story. Some parts of it, she declared, "made her tremble in her shoes while she sat."

Mr. Guttle, as he left the house, was met by Miss Figginbottom, who was coming, full of wrath and vengeance against Miss Charlotte Dibbs, having discovered it to have been her who placed the jallop in Mrs. Dibbs's tea-pot; thereby causing much pain and fright to her (Miss Figginbottom) and many others.

"So, Miss!" exclaimed she, as with virtuous indignation she strided into the room, "So, Miss! I rather think I have you now: who put physic in the tea?"

"Lor! sister Figginbottom," said Mrs. Dibbs, you surely don't mean to say 'twas her!"

"But I do, though, Mrs. Dibbs," returned the indignant Miss Figginbottom, "here 's the druggist she had it of, ready to take his oath;" and Miss Figginbottom drew up her head, and looked very stately indeed.

"Then you're done, old girl!" said Miss Charlotte, "for I had it from his wife."

Now, Miss Figginbottom had merely mentioned the affair of the druggist on speculation; and when Miss Charlotte was thus caught in a trap of her own setting, she became very much delighted indeed: in fact, in her joy, she almost forgot to fly out at being addressed as "old girl." Miss Figginbottom is not the only aged lady who is tenacious of her youth. "He-he," simpered she, "he-he-he; really, very good indeed! so you got it from the wife, did you! nice young lady, indeed! Why, if I was Mrs. Dibbs, I'd tear your eyes out; I would, and no mistake. Hey-day, indeed, things is come to a pretty pass: what next, I should like to know; yes, I should only like to know what next. Oh, you little beast!" Having thus delivered herself, Miss Figginbottom stalked out of the house, leaving Mrs. Dibbs uncertain as to the manner in which she should administer punishment to her niece: how she longed to flog her; but how would that agree with her affectation of gentleness? and the problem remained unsolved when a letter arrived for Mrs. Dibbs, with which that lady was not a little astonished.

CHAPTER IV.

A DISCLOSURE.—A MIDNIGHT WEDDING.

MRS. DIBBS received information, in this letter, that a woman, supposed to be dying in the village, prayed instantly to see her. She obeyed the summons; and, at her return, she made a communication to Mrs. Gapper, which, coming from her, much surprised that worthy lady.

Mrs. Dibbs had been the confidential servant of Constance Hastings; and she was fully aware of the circumstances which her friend, through Mr. Guttle, had already become acquainted with.

Mrs. Hastings, we know, at her death, left two daughters, joint-heiresses of the estates of Learmont, under the guardianship of her husband. The elder of these children was stolen, while yet an infant; and all enquiries regarding her fate, having proved fruitless, her sister had long been considered as sole heiress to her grandfather's enormous wealth.

Mr. Hastings, too, had for some years, poor man, been dead; and it was not until many efforts, which had happily been frustrated, had, nevertheless, been made against the life of the little Constance, that Mrs. Dibbs consented, at the advice in council of the most sapient of her friends, to hide, for a time, her little charge, until she should be of a better age to protect, and obtain protectors for, herself.

And thus, in obscurity, under the name of her nurse, grew up this young lady, whose tendency to mischievous propensities we have already spoken of with regret.

It was, doubtless, with much satisfaction that the Last of the Vampires had beheld the obstructions between the Castle of Learmont and himself thus gradually disappear. The eldest daughter stolen, with the assistance of a servant, from the parental roof, we have already seen wither and die, blasted by cruelty, like a tender plant before the east wind, in the Castle Von Oberfels.

Of many of these particulars Mrs. Dibbs had been ignorant, until the death-bed confession she had then heard of a fellow-servant, had put her in possession of the whole.

* * * * *

It wanted one hour to midnight: in the hall of a German castle stood a goodly bridal procession, waiting only for the fair presence of the bride. The Baron Von Oberfels was there, once more arrayed in the garments of a bridegroom. It was with somewhat of anxiety that, ever and anon, he raised his eyes towards a large clock. It was the greatest risk he had ever run; for there he read, that in less than one short hour, the sand in his glass would have run out for ever; and as horrible thoughts would rise to his mind, which he could not repress, he suffered truly the torments of the condemned. The bride at length appeared, and the procession moved forward towards the ancient chapel, and the ceremony began.

At the front of the altar (Oh, profane mockery!) knelt the baron and his victim; behind, the friends of the latter, attired in all the pomp and gorgeousness of days gone by, stood round in a semi-circle, the torches of the retainers flashing with treble lustre in the brilliant jewels which adorned the guests. The grand organ, pealing forth some sacred harmony, was accompanied by the heavenly voices of the white-robed choristers, whose notes, as they swelled, and sank, and died away in the distance, added greatly to the beauty of the scene. But hark! another noise is heard; sulphureous smoke half fills the sacred building; the floor opens for an instant; and mocking shrieks are audible, as the spirit of the Last of the Vampires descended into perdition.

SEQUEL.

SOMEWHERE about the commencement of the present century, a gentleman, who was acquainted with all the events detailed before, put up to rest his horse at the Nag's Head, in the village of Frampton: his numerous enquiries to the waiter were answered by that official, nearly as follows:

Mrs. Gapper?

A lady of that name, who married a certain Mr. Guttle, was, with her husband, still living in the place.

And Miss Hastings?

That young lady, now on the point of marriage, was residing at the seat of her ancestors: the faithful Dibbs was, however, dead; and Constance, as she daily strived to obtain the education of which she had hitherto been destitute, would often drop a tear to the memory of her unfortunate Gertrude.

The Rev. Ptolemy Huggins?

That gentleman, having become the husband of Miss Figginbottom, had been hurried, by her temper, into an untimely grave, whither she, herself, had nearly followed him.

Of the fate of Marie Flors, history is silent. The Castle Oberfels has reverted to the Crown: but, as yet, no one has been found of sufficient boldness to enter the deserted castle of—

THE LAST OF THE VAMPIRES.

FINIS.